D0044165

THE REVIVAL

THE REVIVAL

BY

CHRIS WEITZ

LITTLE, BROWN AND COMPANY

New York Boston

Copyright © 2016 by Chris Weitz
3-D type by Michael-Paul Terranova

Little, Brown and Company

Hachette Book Group
1290 Avenue of the Americas, New York, NY 10104
Visit us at lb-teens.com

Little, Brown and Company is a division of Hachette Book Group, Inc.
The Little, Brown name and logo are trademarks of Hachette Book Group, Inc.

First Edition: July 2016

ISBN 978-0-316-22634-9

10 9 8 7 6 5 4 3 2 1

RRD-C

Printed in the United States of America

For Athena

DONNA

THE STEADY DRONE OF HELICOPTER blades and military jargon might put me in a meditative frame of mind, if my heart weren't beating louder than any other sound, because New York, beautiful New York, hideous New York, is stretched ahead of us, the thick ribbon of Manhattan joined loosely to the mainland and the nub of Long Island by thin threads of bridge.

Somewhere in those canyons and alleys, I hope, is Jefferson.

The damage is hard to see from up here. We dive down for a lower pass, and Colonel Wakefield talks to me over the headphones.

Wakefield: "It doesn't look too bad. I don't see a problem with Zone A."

Zone A is Central Park.

Me: "I'm telling you, it's better to go to Randall's Island." I search my mind for the correct jargon. "Zone C. There's no way of knowing what's going down in the park, I mean Zone A. You could have loonies with bows and arrows hiding out in the bushes. Things get pretty real down there."

Wakefield: "I think we should just about manage."

This is the British understatement thing, which is cute and all, but it doesn't fill me with the confidence it's supposed to. I get where he's coming from—these are some major ass-kickers I'm traveling with. SAS stands for Special Air Service, which sounds like they're really great flight attendants or something, but in fact the SAS are the most killer-y of killers selected from the British armed forces, a group already loaded chock-full of working-class guys with attitude problems. People like to think of the Brits as sophisticated and everything, all umbrellas and tea and stuff, but a pint glass smashed into your face at closing time is probably more representative of the population as a whole. The officers are even more scary because they *seem* all genteel but they're every bit as ready-to-eat-bugs-and-jam-their-thumbs-into-your-eyes as the rest.

I look down the line of jump seats and see the Gurkhas. Little smiley guys with big curved knives. By reputation they're the most dangerous of the lot.

Rab catches my eye and holds up three fingers, which means *channel three*. He wants a private moment on a separate channel from the others.

I've been ignoring him so far. But it's getting to be more trouble than it's worth.

Me: "Yeah?"

Rab: "I just want you to know that I agree with you."

Me: "Well, as we used to say, that and three bucks gets me a ride on the subway."

Rab: "Getting back into a New York state of mind, I see."

I'm not really in the mood for banter.

Me: "What do you want?" I can't even say his name.

Rab: "You're thinking about *him*. Jefferson."

I'm annoyed that he's even bringing this up. Maybe I'm a little ashamed. Maybe he's putting it out there, like, *If we do find Jefferson, I'm going to tell him we've been sleeping together, and spoil your little reunion.*

I look over at Rab, the honey trap, the muscley shoulder to cry on. The government informer. The spy. The liar.

Rab: "I'm sorry. They made me do it."

Me: "Not half as sorry as I am." *They made me do it.* That's nice.

Rab: "I wanted to tell you. I still—"

I jump back to channel one. No interest in rehashing that stuff. I suppose you have to admire the guy for trying. What does he want? Is there something else he can get out of me? Or does he really want to make amends, to, what, "get back together"? I look away, which takes a little doing, since he's nice to look at. But it's so over.

Poor Donna, deceived by a dude, all alone in a box of bros. Working for the Man.

My mind turns again to the gender politics of this race to secure the nukes. I'm thinking how all up and down the line, the guys running this show, not to mention the Reconstruction Committee, are, you know, guys.

I used to think I was a feminist. I was all, *Girl power!* and stuff. Figured that if I didn't take any shit, that pretty much counted as, like, my contribution to society. But when I look back and examine my actions, I was mostly going with the flow. A lot of the time when I thought I was being awesome and *Equal*? I was just making token resistance, a sort of Aunt Thomasina.

I look around the cabin, full of broken noses and swollen knuckles, and I think, *Maybe men and women are individual, but symbiotic, species?* I mean, what if back in the primordial soup, before sexual reproduction, everything was just fine and then that Y chromosome snuck in and made half the population brutal and slutty?

But how to even up the score? How to be a real feminist, post-apocalyptically speaking?

The chopper makes a hard right toward Central Park, the cabin tilting, the squaddie next to me practically crushing me. "Sorry, miss," he says, but he cops a feel as he slides back down the bench.

For the past few years of my life, this has been the deal—a lot of people with dicks and guns doing whatever they like.

Life back at Washington Square, our tribe's home, had been, again theoretically, more fair. I mean, there's nothing like the end of civilization for a reboot of society. But even there, it was a bro running the show. I loved Washington as much as anybody else. But still. Sometimes I think a girl like me might have run things better, nome sane?

The helicopter backs and hovers, whipping up dirt and chaff from the ground through the cold air, and the SAS guys give their kit one last check, all their nylon war-fetish gear, their matte-black knives and carabiners and nylon loops and snub automatics.

Maybe this is how it works. Maybe the road to equality is not paved with good intentions and laid on a foundation of law and gradual social change. Maybe it's seized at gunpoint.

The helicopter sets down as light as can be, the rotors flattening the tall brown grass outward into an undulating crop circle. Out pour the commandos, ten from each of the two troop choppers, plus myself, my gigantic minder, Titch, and my lying-sack-of-shit ex-briefly-boyfriend, Rab. A third helicopter, a giant number with two rotors, disgorges its cargo like big rectangular poops and heads back to the east, where the carrier group is waiting in the Long Island Sound.

The moon is only a semicircular gouge of light, so the world is dark gray, with the lumps of granite and shaggy outlines of trees giving way to blocky rectangles of apartment buildings shouldering over the park walls in the distance.

I know who lives there.

Uptown.

The helicopter has given away the game. By now everybody above Fifty-Ninth Street has probably seen us and realized that, contrary to what they thought, the rest of the world is not mired in a post-apocalyptic goatfuck like they are. I can't imagine they're taking it in stride. They will be awakening, with a jolt, from a nightmare into a world of infinite possibilities.

Sheep Meadow is even more sketch than it was the last time I was here. Overgrown and stuck in winter, it looks like the landscape equivalent of a drug-addicted drifter who hasn't showered in a month.

Last time—those were the days! Jefferson and I were young and infected and Not Dead Yet, trekking north, stalked by Uptowners and polar bears. Aiming to save the world, or at least ourselves, with a cure for the Sickness. And damned if we didn't do it, minus one or two fatalities.

SeeThrough. Kath.

Wakefield: "So far, so good."

He means that he was right and I was wrong, and the shitstorm of Hurricane Sandy proportions that I had been expecting hasn't materialized. The park does seem quiet.

Wakefield: "We'll make our way east to the UN and, with any luck, the football."

"The football" is the launch codes and activation device for the US Strategic Nuclear Arsenal. So, you know, kind of a big deal.

That's what we're here for. It's a big black leather satchel, *very* dowdy and unstylish, like total substitute teacher gear, with a leather loop attached to the handle that goes around your arm. Or rather, a military officer's arm. It was that person's job to hover in the vicinity of the president at all times, waiting around just in case somebody felt like setting off a global thermonuclear war. At such time, the president had his handy-dandy launch authorizations nearby to call in to CentCom via a special satphone— "the biscuit"—and authorize the end of the world, or at least the next best thing.

Wakefield continues, "We should be able to fend off any sporadic attacks in the meanwhile."

Me: "Colonel, everybody on this island is gonna want to find out who you are, and how you managed to live this long, and whether you've got a cure for the Sickness. That means *thousands* of desperate, armed people."

Wakefield: "Children."

Me: "Who have survived here for years. Unlike you."

He looks at me skeptically, as though making a Mental Note in his Mental Notebook, which is probably, by the way, Mentally

Matte Black. I wonder how many generations of military types have ignored the advice of their native guides—which is more or less what I am—and how many people have gotten killed as a result.

Wakefield: "That's not my concern."

It is, I understand, beyond the scope of his interest, which is to say it has nothing to do with the mission to get the football.

Guja: "Miss Donna, you are doing okay?" He's a little man—shorter than me, at least, and I barely top five feet—with a wide and ready smile. Calling him *little* might make him sound less than formidable, but Guja is a Gurkha, from this brigade of Nepalese soldiers who've served in the British army for over two hundred years.

Story was, the British, who in that particular century were traipsing around the globe trying to subjugate anybody brown they found along the way, hit a speed bump when they came across this one tribe. The Gurkhas hadn't opened the e-mail about cringing before the awesome spectacle of Victorian tech and discipline. They were all, like, *Come at me, bro*. The Brits were so impressed they hired them.

Guja and the other Gurkhas are hacking away at the long grass of Central Park with their kukris, which are these long, curved knives that look like sharpened metal boomerangs. Now he's taken a break from punishing the local flora to ask after me.

I like Guja, but I also know why he and the other Gurkhas make up half the team. It's because they take orders and kill without question and have just about zero sense of connection to teenage New Yorkers who, to be fair, probably have zero affinity for Nepalese tribesmen.

Me: "Okay, Guja."

But really, nothing is okay. Okayness is definitely in short supply. I'm back in the suck. After a brief interlude in Cambridge, where for a while I had even convinced *myself* that I was just a normal survivor of the American diaspora, stuff got, once again, F'd up, like beyond F'd up, practically G'd up or H'd up.

I glance at Rab. He's pushing back his magazine-shoot hair and hefting crates and boxes from the helicopter to stack them outside, trying to fit in with the Gurkhas and the hard-faced SAS commandos. I could almost feel sorry for him, pretty boy among all these stony military types.

When I met him in Cambridge, I thought he was part of the student Resistance, protesting the social controls that the government and the American Reconstruction Committee had placed on the populace. Restrictions on speech, movement, ideology. Behind a façade of normal life, they had eyes and ears on everything at all times. You were even monitored from your own pocket—every cell phone an informant.

And me? I was just a little citrus fruit they wanted to squeeze for information. I'd been at the UN, you see, the day that the

9

president died. So they figured I had information about the football.

Anyway, Rab wasn't working for the Resistance after all. He was working for the government.

He smiles at me, shrugs, like *Who am I kidding?* and saunters over from the piles of gear. His face registers determination. Once-more-into-the-breach kind of thing.

Rab: "I never thought I'd end up here. Did you? That night in the bar?"

The scene: the college bar, a lonely American girl far from home, nursing a Budweiser. In steps Rab, all raven-haired and copper-skinned beauty, limestone-green eyes, the whole package. Begin a friendship tinged with attraction. Cut the cord connecting the girl to her friends, telling her they're dead. American girl falls into the ready arms of the new friend and tells all— everything she knows about her dark past in post-catastrophe New York. Government gets what it wants.

Rab is still waiting for an answer to his question.

Me: "No, I guess I never thought I'd be back in New York."

I was ready to stay in Cambridge. On some level, I *knew* that Rab was too good to be true. I was broken and falling and looking for a soft place to land. Someone to listen. A good time. A little happiness. So sue me.

His hand wanders toward mine. There is a thrill—but it's just some stupid emo neurons that haven't gotten the memo, firing for no good reason. I pull away. Turn my back.

Jefferson is somewhere out there. I hope.

Me: "Cut it out."

Rab: "Donna. This is the right side. Us." I'm not sure if he means him and the rest of the Brits, or him and me.

Me: "See, that's your problem. The moment I think you're getting real, it gets all political."

Rab: "I want you to be safe, that's why. If Jefferson is alive—" He's taken aback by the contempt on my face. "And I hope he is, for your sake," he adds. "If he's alive, then he's in the company of some dangerous, irresponsible people."

He means the Resistance. Specifically, Chapel.

Me: "Wow. You really drank the Kool-Aid, huh? Or did Welsh tell you to say that?"

Rab: "You think the Resistance wants to save everybody. I get it. That's why they used you. But they don't care about distributing the Cure. All they want is the nukes. And if they get them, they're going to send the world back to the Stone Age."

Me: "Bullshit."

Except maybe he's right. Chapel came on very idealistic and self-sacrificing, like he wanted to save all of us post-apocalyptic little mofos. Otherwise we wouldn't have helped him. But something about this whole affair—down to my getting used by the government—makes me think that nobody in this game is innocent.

Except Jefferson. Of everyone I know, he's the one who would hold on to his principles. *He* would never compromise.

The gear has been unloaded, but we're still just standing around at the landing site. I want to get going. Go find him. But there's some kind of delay, a general milling about and grimacing among the SAS guys that, to me, indicates a hitch in our plans. I hear voices raised near one of the helicopters.

I've had enough of this. I walk over to the lead chopper.

The metal cowling is open, and a squaddie is peering in and fiddling with a bit of the engine, a little flashlight (they call them torches, which is cute, very *Minecraft*) clenched between his teeth like a cigar, freeing up both hands. He notices me watching him and contorts his face into a smile without removing the flashlight. The light blinds me for a moment.

Squaddie: "All right, miss?" (Or rather, "Aawwight, mih?")

The squaddies are polite and respectful on the surface, despite their gnarly lifestyle. Seems like they get shipped around to various foreign locales to kick down doors, stab people in the neck, and blow insurgents' brains out from preposterous distances, then get put back on the leash and run through obstacle courses for a rest. They are thoroughly under control, like dogs that can balance a treat on their nose until ordered to eat. Still, they can't seem to stop themselves from eye-boning me, which is surprising since I'm wearing a bulky green jumpsuit a few sizes too big. I guess they don't see too many girls.

I give him a little wave and a shy "Hi!" Despite the fact that I've probably seen more death and destruction than your most hard-bitten special ops special-opper, I'd rather have the squaddies believe that I'm a helpless little waif. It muddies up their suspicions and allows me to slip back into the body of the helicopter unregarded.

The cabin is gloomy, illuminated only by some yellowish LED strips plastered haphazardly here and there. It takes me a while to find what I'm looking for, especially since I have to shift things around as quietly as possible.

Finally, I locate it, a snub orange plastic device that looks like a cartoonish toy pistol. I take some flares from the box and slip it into a pocket of my jumpsuit.

They didn't give me a gun, probably because they don't think I'd know how to use one. Or maybe because they think, if I did know how to use one, I'd just as soon use it on them. Trust has been in pretty short supply since my shenanigans on the flight deck of the *Ronald Reagan*, when I helped the others escape.

But that's not what I want the flare gun for. I hop from the chopper and raise it above my head and fire. As the pink light streaks upward, the overgrown meadow around us is, for a moment, caught in a garish, ruddy glow. We're a lit diorama, a night shoot, a rave, and I can see the confused expressions on everyone's faces.

Swearing and shouting.

Wakefield: "Put that down. *Now.*"

He nods to one of the Gurkhas, who sprints toward me.

I have the second flare in my left hand and jam it quickly into the breech. The heat from the first charge sears my fingers.

I take aim at the moon and pull the trigger. *WHOOMF.* The second flare goes up, burning a line in the sky, the two residual smoke trails making a V with its point on our location.

The Gurkha tackles me, and the air hisses out of my lungs. Up goes the kukri, and I see the bent blade glimmer in the light of the second flare.

Wakefield: "Stop!"

The knife pauses in the air, suspended like a second moon. Guja comes up behind his man and gives him an order in Nepali. The man stands up and raises me by the collar.

Guja looks at me, his smile gone like it never was there.

Guja: "Why, miss? Why?"

I realize that I may have been his particular responsibility just now, and I may have gotten him in some deep shit.

Me: "Sorry, Gooj."

Even if he cared about the answer, how could I explain? That I had a feeling that somewhere out there Jefferson would see, that somehow he would know it was me? That he would come for me and we'd be together again?

JEFFERSON

THROUGH THE FROST-RIMMED WINDOW, I see the flares die down, but the hope remains. A ghostly pink V has taken shape over the park, pointing the way.

We're holed up in a dentist's office in Midtown on what should be called the thirteenth floor but is labeled the fourteenth out of a retrospectively ironic desire to avoid bad luck. Peter lolls on the ground, nursing his heartbreak. The twins leaf through old copies of *Highlights*, looking for Goofus and Gallant cartoons. Kath sits next to Brainbox, who's laid out on the couch.

"Let's go," I say.

"What if it's *not* somebody come to help?" says Kath, her lips twisted in a skeptical moue. At least I'm pretty sure that's what they call it. A distortion that reminds you of the beauty of the original form.

"If it's not, what do we have to lose?" I say.

"Everything," says Kath. "Half the city probably wants to kill you."

"Thanks to you and Theo," I say. There's been no sign of Theo, the Harlemite who went to the lab with us, and then to the carrier, and then on the helicopter back home. Whatever he did after he and Kath exposed my lies at the UN, we've had no word.

"Don't blame Theo, who had a legitimate beef with you, and don't blame *me*, either. I didn't *force* you to lie to everybody," Kath says. "I didn't force you to hide the truth."

"If they knew that..." I search for the right word, choosing the most useful one. "...*civilization* had survived, there'd be a massacre. Everybody would be rushing for the exit out of here."

"That's what *Chapel* said, right? The guy who stole the World's Most Important Briefcase?" She looks over at Peter, who registers the feeling you get when you unexpectedly hear the name of somebody who dumped you. "Sorry," Kath says.

"Even if he's a liar about everything else, he was right about one thing. Haven't you heard the gunshots? The screams? The explosions out there? It's anarchy."

Kath shrugs. "Right. Which is why we should sit tight. Everybody's losing their minds. You remember what that random said? Everybody's heading down to Battery Park."

"There's a big boat coming to pick everybody up!" says Anna, the girl twin, brightly.

"There's no boat," I say. "Well, there is, but it's not coming for us. It's a nuclear-powered aircraft carrier, and they'd just as soon carpet bomb this place. I don't trust the Reconstruction Committee."

"But you trust whoever shot those flares? That's weak."

I don't tell her that, deep inside, I have a hope, which is becoming a conviction, that it's Donna who shot those flares. It doesn't make any sense. But the feeling is there nonetheless.

"So stay. I'm going to find out who it was." I shoulder my pack.

Kath looks like she doesn't buy my indifference. And it's true, she's a hard person to be indifferent about, even if she has completely screwed up my life. There's her beauty, of course, the ridiculous plummy ripeness of her. But it's more than that. There's a sort of gravitational quality to her spirit, like a cliff edge that you can't help but peek over. And some part of me always wants to jump. Thanatos, they used to call it—the death wish.

"Is that any way to thank me for saving your life?" Kath continues with a smile.

That's technically true. Once everyone else found out about the Cure, I was lucky to escape with my skin intact. Kath and the Thrill Kill Twins pulled me out, along with Brainbox and Peter, through the cloaca of the UN compound.

"You killed me," I counter. "You started the lynch mob that's after me." Now we're hiding by day, moving by night, waiting for the peasants with pitchforks and torches.

"Don't be a drama queen. They would have found out you were lying soon enough."

"I just needed a little time. I wanted something better. For everybody."

"Yeah, I know." Kath smirks. "You're cute. I bet that big get-together you organized gave you a raging Righteousness Boner. You got to play Model UN. Even write a constitution."

I wanted to establish some kind of structure before the adults came. According to Chapel, they were just waiting for us to die off. So it seemed to me the best thing to do was to band together. After all, we had the Cure. We could start again. And we could organize to defend ourselves against whoever was coming once the rest of the world realized that we were staying for the long haul.

"But guess what?" Kath says. "Given the choice, given the *facts*, people didn't want to be part of your Utopia. They wanted Wi-Fi."

"If you think I'm so naive, then what are you doing here?"

I still can't figure it. It was one thing for her to take revenge. After all, I broke up with her. If you can really use a banal term like that in a world that comprehends plague and cannibalism. And I left her for dead.

Of course, I didn't know she wasn't *actually* dead. Not that she didn't hold it against me.

But by hanging around, she's put herself in danger, too.

At that, Kath actually seems kind of stumped. Or as though she doesn't want to say. Finally, she shrugs.

"Nothing better to do. But that doesn't mean I want to waltz around outside asking to get shot."

"It's your own damn people that's gonna do it," says Peter, reminding Kath of her Uptown roots.

"Yeah, my *former* own damn people. I'm not exactly beloved out there." She raises her eyebrows (plucked, somehow, even under these circumstances) for emphasis. "Look, I'm not just thinking for myself any longer. I've got two kids."

She means the Long Islanders she picked up at the lab, tow-headed twins named Anna and Abel but who she calls the Thrill Kill Twins. The springy little blue-eyed ectomorphic psychotics follow Kath's instructions to the letter, which is what they did for the Old Man before I killed him. I can't tell if Kath really cares about them or if her protectiveness is an elaborate running gag on her part. Maybe she can't tell, either.

"I'm heading toward those flares," I say. "I bet it's the adults. It might be military, it might be the Resistance, but whoever it is, they're our best shot at helping Brainbox. If we don't get him some medical attention soon..."

I don't finish the thought. I don't want Brainbox to hear, if he's even conscious.

His stomach has stopped bleeding. There's a neat little hole where Chapel shot him, about four inches to the left of his belly button, surrounded by flesh so pallid it could be a fish's stomach instead of a kid's. No exit wound. I think that's not a good thing. Like maybe the bullet bounced around inside him, or expanded as it traveled through his guts. They designed them to do that. His breathing is shallow and fast, his pulse irregular. His body is slick with oily sweat.

Donna would know what to do about it. She was the tribe's doctor, since she practically grew up in the ER where her mom was a nurse. She would manage to whip up some kind of treatment from the dentist's shelves. Now it's been two days and I've run out of bright ideas. We found some expired novocaine and shot him up. Beyond that, I'm out of answers, at a point of absolute stasis. Like a marble at the bottom of a bowl—no kinetic energy left for me to move anywhere. At least I was, until I saw the flares.

"Jefferson's right. We need to make a move. I'll help," says Peter. He literally shakes off his grief over Chapel's betrayal—wagging his head like he can dispose of his thoughts by flinging them centrifugally out of his brain.

Kath gets up, too. "Fine," she says. "I always hated the dentist's anyway. C'mon, kids." She nudges the twins in the ribs, and they sit up, clearing the muck from their eyes.

"What now, Mommy?" says Anna. Though she's maybe fourteen, she acts much younger. Her malnourished frame makes it even more creepy.

"I'm not your mommy," says Kath, a routine they go through. Then, "We're going to the park."

"Yay!" says Abel.

We do a weapons check. Kath has a Mauser pistol with fifteen rounds. Peter and I still have our AR-15s, with a few magazines of ammunition to spare. The twins are down to a crowbar with duct-tape handle and a Louisville Slugger. Not much to go on, but it's all we have.

Downstairs, the street is abandoned, but we can hear activity nearby—the dawn chorus of gunshots and screams. I can see my breath, and as we exit the building, snowflakes start to fall, appearing like a quintessence of the air, like it's supersaturated with ice.

The winter will be ugly. Last year, we burned everything we could and still lost people to the cold that crept up on us while we slept, extinguishing fires and lives.

We hustle along with a folded-over bedsheet taut between us, carrying Brainbox and some of our gear. He clutches the biscuit, the nuclear trigger, close to his chest. He's half awake and mumbling something over and over again. It sounds like "Chrysanthemum, Chrysanthemum." But that makes no sense. Maybe it's some kind of chemical formula.

We have to move quickly before we lose the darkness. Every second, nature turns the brightness up a little more, and we're more exposed. The snow starts blotting out the blackness, and we slip on the film of white that starts to coat the ground.

The quickest way to the park is through Uptowners' territory, a zigzag stair-stepping diagonal to East Fifty-Ninth Street and Fifth Avenue. A dangerous mile to the site of the flares.

"I don't suppose you'd like to hit the subway?" asks Peter, scanning the surrounding buildings, any of which could house a lookout with a sniper rifle. He has his own gun at the ready, but there's no way we can cover all the angles.

I don't even answer. The subway holds evil memories: headlong flight through the blind darkness, loss, and massacre. I'd rather die in the light.

We totter up Third Avenue, past the shells of dead banks, their plate-glass windows long ago smashed, the ATMs scraped empty when money still meant something. Chain restaurants picked clean, stores looted, angry irregular cubes of shattered glass crunching underfoot. Cars siphoned. An urban landscape scoured free of everything useful.

We avoid the wide lanes of Fifty-Ninth and head west on Six-tieth, which is lined with shrines to anachronism: a nail bar, a car-pet store, a tailor. From here, it's a quick jog across Park Avenue, Brainbox moaning as each step jars him. At the corner, there's a stubby sandstone-and-brick building. A tattered banner says this was Christ Church Day School.

I notice Kath has stopped. She's staring up at the banner.

"What is it?" I say.

"I went here," she says. "We played up on the roof. See the cage around the edge?"

To keep balls, and children, from flying off and falling to the street below.

"I didn't know your family was religious," I say.

"We weren't religious," she says. "We were rich. That's what this school was for. Not God. Money." She continues, strangely philosophical, "If your parents spent the money to get you in here, then you got the kind of education to get you into the next place. Chapin, Nightingale, Brearley, Buckley, Collegiate. And then maybe you could get into the Ivies. And then you could get into one of the big firms. Or work at the Met so you had stuff to talk about at cocktail parties and could meet the right people. Then you could marry somebody who was important enough or hot enough or rich enough and you could keep the whole cycle going. World without end. Amen."

She says it flatly, without acid, downright alkaline.

"I'm glad it's all over," she says. "Let's get out of here."

As we walk along, we come to a little stoop and she says, "The nannies would wait for us here. The third world, like, waiting for the first. If you didn't know the deal, you might think they were moms here to pick up their kids. You might think that there were lots of interracial marriages here on the Upper East Side. Ha.

"My parents always had to take everything a step further, so our nanny was Swiss. None of that Hispanic stuff for them. We were supposed to call her *mademoiselle*. But she didn't seem like a *miss*; she was big and brawny and strict, so we called her Madame Muscle."

I try to talk her out of her reverie. "She was mean to you?"

Kath shakes her head. "She was kind to us. She loved us. I think my parents didn't like that. Made them feel inadequate. Which they were. Then Madame Muscle got a funny lump in her breast. Then my parents fired her. Maybe they fired her first. I forget. Anyway, we never heard from her again. Or rather, she never heard from us. We asked to see her, but my parents wouldn't take us to the hospital."

She looks up and catches my expression. Dismisses my sympathy. "Boo-hoo, I can hear the world's smallest violin playing. There. Almost made it."

She's looking ahead. We can see the trees of the park reaching over the walls. A sprint and we'd make it, but we still have Brainbox slung between us, and there's only so fast we can go.

The Uptowners are waking. The first sign that we've been spotted is a water balloon breaking in front of us. We look up and see a kid flipping us the bird. Where the balloon hit, a noxious smell erupts.

Then Peter is hit by another one. It explodes on his shoulder and splashes the side of his head. His hands go to his eyes, and he screams in pain as I duck the drops that scatter into the air.

"Pepper spray!" he says before Kath and I drag him toward the building, under its big elaborate eaves. It's an old building, made with care. Tall sash windows, sandstone and curlicues. More balloons hit the ground.

We crowd against a mottled bronze sign that reads THE METRO-POLITAN CLUB: 1891.

"Oh shit," says Kath when she realizes.

"Oh shit, what?"

"I wasn't thinking. This place...We should've gone another way."

"Why?"

"It used to be a private club. Like, old dudes backslapping and drinking. Now it's basically a barracks."

As she says this, I hear a commotion from beyond a set of high metal gates. Uptowners are swarming out of an ornamental vestibule, carrying guns, bats, swords, knives, pouring out like poison.

I crook my AR through the bars of the gate and fire, sending the frontmost tumbling to the ground and temporarily damming the flow.

"We've got to get away while we have a chance," says Kath. "Leave him here."

She means Brainbox, who, fortunately, isn't conscious to hear it.

"Fuck that," says Peter.

"He comes with us," I say.

"*Fine,*" says Kath, and seizes an edge of the sheet and starts trotting ahead, practically pulling Brainbox out of my hands.

We totter toward the park as the Uptowners gather their courage and pursue. But before we can even cross Fifth, I see a gun barrel pointing over the low wall ahead of us. Guards in the park start firing, swearing, and launching steel arrows that clank along the ground at our feet.

"That way!" I call. We take a left, back toward downtown and the fortress-like Plaza Hotel, with its big mucky fountain out in front and, nearby, a golden equestrian statue striding irrelevantly and perpetually forward. A glance tells me that this, too, is a bad

25

scene—the hotel's flagpoles are draped in private school banners, and armed thugs loiter on the steps.

We switch direction again, find ourselves backed against a glass cube projecting from the ground. Sci-fi glass architecture with a familiar logo etched above a transparent portal: a giant apple with a bite out of it.

I remember pictures of people lining up for days, sleeping on the streets, waiting for the advent of the new iPhone. Urban campers. Bougies in a breadline for one of the few things they couldn't yet have.

"Ugh. Retail," says Kath. She's actually thinking of facing the mob rather than fleeing into the Apple Store.

"At least it's a flagship store," I say.

I wedge the doors open—the mechanical opener is long dead— and help the others pull Brainbox through. As we get him to the bottom of the spiral glass stairs, the Uptowners thunder down after us. It's the Thrill Kill Twins who save the day. They charge up the stairs and flail away at our pursuers with their makeshift clubs. One Uptowner and then another falls, until the entryway is clogged with broken bodies, and the rest retreat. The twins gallop down the stairs, faces dotted with blood and smiles flashing.

We collapse in a pile behind the rattling metal gate, a utilitarian embarrassment that never would have been seen during opening hours. It runs the length of the basement vestibule and serves, effectively, to wall us off from the world above. We throw the bolts at the edges and find ourselves, for the moment, safe.

I shut the padlocks on the bolt housings. I have no idea where to find the keys, so there's no getting out, but that seems to me the least of our problems.

"What is this place?" asks Abel, the boy twin, and that's how I know he must really be traumatized. He can't be so young that he doesn't know about iPhones and MacBooks, but he's been through so much that those memories have been wiped from his mind.

"It's an Apple Store."

"I don't see any apples."

His eyes are bright and empty, his face freckled with drying gore. Back at the lab on Plum Island, the Old Man had a whole school class of tweens like this one under his control, stoked with amphetamines, tranquilizers, and video games.

I hope these children are not the future.

The Uptowners have now gotten down the stairs and are smashing at the gate like something out of *The Walking Dead*. They perforate the slats with bullets, and I pull the others to the ground before anyone gets hurt. Next to me, little elfin Anna chortles, like this is all a game.

Thin shafts of light pierce the murk. It reminds me of ten or twenty movies I've seen but can't put a name to. Then I think of how strange it is to think your life evokes a moment in a film, and I tell myself, no, this moment, maybe one of my last moments, belongs to me, and it reminds me of nothing. This moment reminds me only of itself.

There's a lull as the Uptowners try to figure a way to pry the metal gate open and realize it won't be an easy task. We can see them eyeballing us through the bullet holes.

"You're gonna die!" they shout. "Shoulda never come Uptown, bitches!" And then they just start to howl.

We could answer back if there were anything useful to say. But we've given up on words. Instead, we've fallen into some vestigial mode of hunter and prey; they may as well be badgers digging up a rabbit's nest.

I can't help feeling that it'll get worse.

EVAN

I LOOK AROUND AT THE OYSTER BAR, the bros sitting in council, the white Formica stained with brown blood, the prisoner and me in the hollow of the U-shaped counter.

Pap! I backhand the kid again. Actually, he's not a kid; he's an adult. He just looks like a little pussy-ass bitch, so we thought he was young. He's been ready to talk for a while, but I'm angry and I'm high and I'm having fun and he's the nearest thing to hurt. Besides, he's got to know what's what and who's who, for instance who runs this bitch. Which is me. And it's not just him that's got to know that I am not suddenly fuckwithable, new developments notwithstanding. The whole Confederacy has got to know, all the captains, all the bros, all the bitches.

Ever since we found out that little shit Jefferson was lying to us and that there were actually old people out there in the big, wide world, and they still had, like, iPhones or whatever, people have been peeling off, trying to find some magical rescue party they think is coming to save them.

I'm maybe not as enthusiastic as everybody else about the news, and I've made it clear that defection from the Confederacy will be punishable by death, but still, motherfuckers be slippin'. Problem is, maybe I apply the death penalty to too many things, like, people figure, I'm probably gonna get popped for some other bullshit anyway, so I may as well split now.

That's what you call a perverse incentive.

It's a fine line between fun and long-term damage, I like to say, so I stop, and I tell him, *Okay, spill*, which doesn't sound as cool as I wanted it to.

He looks at me and says, *Spill? Who are you, Humphrey Bogart?*

I'm like, *Who the hell is that?* but then I remember he was one of my dad's favorites, and he's right, it sounded like an old-timey movie, like some black-and-white shit, and that's kind of hard to pull off. I was hoping for gangster, or rather, gangsta. Next time I kick someone's ass, I'll say something different.

I put a lot of work into the shit I say. Why? Well, in part it's for the bros because, you know, you've got to have a certain amount of style when you're a leader of men like I am.

But when it really comes down to it, I could give two shits what people think of me. What would be the point of an apocalypse if you couldn't be yourself? Like, what's the point of obeying rules when the rules have been thrown out? Make your own rules, like that ad used to say. That's what I'm about. That's how I've crafted this Confederacy, using my personal charisma, my willingness to go the extra mile in terms of inflicting pain when necessary. I'm like Steve Jobs or some shit.

Check it—here's why I am always being stylishly badass and saying awesome things: I'm in a movie that God is watching.

Not an actual movie, of course. Duh. A metaphorical movie. You must have felt it before, right? The sense that somebody was watching, or the desire to behave as though somebody was watching.

So I fancy up my moves a little, beat Chapel with some style, fan my hand back and forth when I slap him.

I think that people had it all wrong about God—that, like, he cares. I mean, yeah, he cares, but not in a *Here, let me help you with that, poor baby* sort of way. I mean, obviously he doesn't give a shit. He cares in a sort of *Wow, I wonder how this episode is going to end* way. Or *I wonder what this character is going to do!* Or *This is getting boring. Time for some action!*

See, God has a whole bunch of universes that he created—and don't say that he couldn't, because that's saying that there's something that God can't accomplish, which is saying that there's something more powerful than God, which is blasphemy, which is wrong.

God is, like, channel surfing between various universes with a big universal remote, just checking things out. Not intervening. When you watch a movie, do you want to have to decide all the time what people do and say, or would you rather be told a story? Would you rather have your team always win, or not know, so that it's exciting when they do? There you go. So God sits back and watches, celestial popcorn in the cup holder of his heavenly La-Z-Boy.

And it's our job not to bore him.

This time around, he wanted excitement and sex and novelty, so he went for a teen apocalyptic action movie.

Makes sense, right? And my point is, it's up to me not to be an extra. Like, I spent so much of my life wondering what it was all about. What the point was. And now I finally found out. It's about me! And the point is me!

Chapel is moaning a little now, but I can't allow myself to lose focus, can't stop kicking ass and looking good and coming up with cool dialogue. Like, I don't want God to get tired of all this. 'Cause if he does, maybe I get canceled.

But you know what? I kind of have a feeling he's into it. I mean, I feel like there's somebody looking out for me, like no matter how hard the haters hate, Evan comes out on top.

Which is so sweet, because all my life up until the Sickness, nobody cared. That is, nobody in authority. They were always trying to trip me up. Like, parents and teachers and shit. Life was just the word *no* over and over again.

No, you can't have that.

No, you can't do that.

Leave your sister alone.

Don't hit him.

Don't grab!

Don't take that!

That's not nice, that's not kind, we're so disappointed, how could you do this to us after all you've been given?

Fuck that noise.

Shit, I'm punching the dude again. I gotta watch that, hurting people without thinking. I take a little walk around the counter, catch my breath, because whaling on this dude takes energy. I look up at the vaulted ceiling, down again at the bros, sitting around the Formica in the old leather swivel chairs like they're waiting for lunch.

I focus my attention on the prisoner.

The guy smiles, which looks creepy since his nose is busted and there's a fine line of blood outlining each of his teeth. He says, *Are you done?*

I think to myself, the guy's got some balls, not like the usual whimpering mess we get down here.

It's nighttime in the Oyster Bar, and I've got center stage as my boys from the various posses of our Uptown Confederacy look on.

33

There's representatives from all the major schools: Buckley, Collegiate, St. Bernard's. They applaud when I stop, flick the blood off my hands, and bow. *Nice one, Evan!*

Sick!

Thought you were going all the way!

They high-five, tilt back their brews, lean over to get a closer look at the prisoner's face.

I take in the compliments, tally who is acting the most loyal.

They're all my boys, but you never know who might have to get kicked off the island.

The atmosphere is kinda tense. This is a closed meeting, soldiers at the door. Inside, it's all quiet and stuff, so quiet you can hear the blood pitter and patter on the floor. Outside, you can hear the party, the one that doesn't stop, over the sounds of the diesel engines. Booze, sex, drugs, fighting. Entertainment. Whatever you want. I love this fucking place. But back to the matter at hand.

Thank you, says the guy, like I've just given him the podium at some conference or something. Like he's not some victim-of-the-day random in the deepest shit of his life.

I think you know the basic facts, he says. *The good news: The rest of the world, outside the US, of course, is free of the Sickness.*

Shouts of amazement from the bros. That's what we've heard from all the rumor-traders and whatnot, but it's another thing to get it from a real live grown-up.

The bad news is, Mommy and Daddy aren't coming to get you. That quiets down the Council. He goes on. *They're going to let you die. Much easier to do that and clear away the corpses than have to deal with all of you twisted little sons of bitches while you're still alive.*

A few of the boys look upset, like downright hurt, at this news. Like they were hoping for a puppy. Like all they want to do is go back to high school and watch YouTube or some shit.

Personally, I'm like, *Forget that.* Have you ever seen that movie *Conan*—the one with Arnold Schwarzenegger, not the one with the Khal Drogo dude? They ask him: Conan, what's the best thing in life, and he's all, *To take no shit, kick major ass, hear your enemies' bitches cry, and party your ass off.* And that's pretty much my zeitgeist or whatever. I was made for this world, and this world was made for me. So I'm not exactly sad that the rescue wagon isn't coming.

Okay, and who are you? I say. I know you're not some kid from the island. You're some kind of spy, right?

I'm Chapel, the guy says, like it's supposed to mean something to me. Then he says, *Lieutenant Commander, US Navy. Well, former.*

Keep going, I say.

Like I said, they're going to let you all die. "They" includes the navy.

35

I'm not dying, I say. *I got the Cure. I got jabbed. You were there.*

Which is true. Down at the United Nations, they had a Gathering of the Tribes. We were supposed to agree to be one big, happy family, and in return, we got the Cure, which was some kind of goo they cooked up from Jefferson's blood. I suppose I've got some of that kid's DNA cruising around my veins. I suppose I owe him my life. I don't like thinking about that.

Chapel shrugs. *Maybe that changes things, maybe not. Probably you're just out of the frying pan and into the fire.*

How do you figure that?

Well, says Chapel, *The Powers That Be—that's the Reconstruction Committee, the US government in exile—figured everybody would be dead in the space of a few years, right? If it turns out that you're going to be playing* Lord of the Flies *in the Big Apple for the next fifty years, let alone* propagating, *they'll change their plans. They'll come in, round you up, and exterminate you.*

Bullshit, says Spencer, one of the capos. *My parents were out of the country when the Sickness hit. If they survived…no way are they gonna just let me die here. Let alone send somebody to kill me.*

I wouldn't be so sure they'll find out you're cured, says Chapel, looking up at all the faces peering at him from around the U-shaped counter. *That's an official secret. Nobody wants to deal with twenty million pimply refugees. The government will keep a lid on the news.*

Above all, they need to keep the Cure from spreading to the rest of the country so they don't have more living teenagers to deal with.

Now this makes me laugh—the idea that somebody would treat the Cure like a disease and try to keep it from spreading. But it makes sense. It's cold, but I get it. Like, if the plan is to take over, who wants somebody like me around, fucking things up? Because no way am I, after the glory years of the Sickness, working for the Man. I'ma carve out my piece of the pie. Each season of The Evan Show has to get cooler and cooler. The budget has to go up; the hero has to rise higher. He has to level up, unlock new powers.

All right, I say to Chapel, *so let 'em come. I got a thousand soldiers. They'll figure out it's better to work with me than against me.*

It's Chapel's turn to laugh, I guess. Which makes me hit him again but probably saves his life because I figure he must know something if he's that ballsy.

Okay, I say, *I'm a busy man. You've got one hundred words to save your life.* This is a favorite game of mine, and the boys know that I like keeping score, so Cooper, from Buckley, takes out a pen and paper. Every once in a while, we'll spark up and do dramatic readings of Famous Last Words and laugh.

Shoot, he says. *I mean, you know what I mean.*

I don't need a hundred words, says Chapel. *Look in the bag.*

Brick—who we named after the dude in *Anchorman* because he's so stupid—brings over the bag Chapel had when he showed up at our doorstep. It's a shitty black leather briefcase stuffed full.

Brick hefts it over and plants it on the counter. I unzip it and empty the contents on the floor. There's a bunch of binders, like in school. They splay open.

So what the hell is this? I say.

That, says Chapel, *is the whole world.*

I pick up the binders and start leafing through the pages. Rows and columns of numbers, some official-looking instructions for a thing that looks, based on the pictures, like an old-fashioned cell phone, from when they were gigantic and crappy.

Doesn't look like the whole world, I say. *Looks like some boring-ass papers.*

You're wrong, he says. *They're the most exciting thing you've ever seen.*

Fuck you, I say. Kind of like somebody else might say, *Oh?*

Let me put it this way, says Chapel. *How would you like to be the most powerful person on the planet?*

You clowning me? Think I'm a punk?

No, says Chapel. *I think you have the launch codes to the United States's strategic nuclear arsenal in your hands.*

I look at the papers again, and it comes into focus.

Holy shit.

Seems too good to be true. *Okay, what makes me so lucky? I mean, you came to us with this.*

Easy, says Chapel. *I need your help. It's going to take some very violent, very unprincipled people to keep me alive through the next few days.*

What do you have planned for the next few days?

See that picture there? Looks like an old walkie-talkie?

I nod. It's a lumpy black piece of hardware.

That's the biscuit, says Chapel. *Whoever has that, and these codes, has control of the biggest nuclear arsenal in the world. That means he has a gun pointed at the head of every man, woman, and child on the face of the globe.*

I like the sound of that. After all, if you can destroy something, that means you control it.

Okay, then where's the biscuit?

Chapel looks, for once, like he's not on top of the world. He says, *Your old buddy Jefferson. Him and his friends.*

Perfect.

So, I say, *we help you get this biscuit thing…*

And I give you the codes.

I don't want to blow everything up.

Well, that's not strictly true. I mean, it would be pretty cool to launch all those missiles. See them streaking through the air as if you were keying the sky like a car door. But what would you do after?

You don't have to, he says. *You just have to convince people you're willing to. And then you can have anything you want. Anything in the world.*

Like I said, somebody up there really likes me. Evan, King of America.

Then one of the soldiers comes in, whispers in my ear the way I told them to do.

We found your sister.

JEFFERSON

AN HOUR LATER AND WE'RE still safe. And still trapped.

Kath and I pace the aisles of the store, looking for something useful. But the laptops and the phones, silvery lozenges propped on the long, altar-like wooden tables, are magics from the past, with nothing to communicate. Are there places where these smooth relics still coax information from the air? Apparently so. Here, they're just oblong slabs of aluminum stuffed with junk.

"Should've listened to me and jettisoned the freak," says Kath. "You've done it this time, cutie."

"Don't call me that."

"Cutie? Why? You don't think you're cute?"

"I don't think I want you to act like things are cool between us."

Kath doesn't seem fazed by this. Unfazability is one of her superpowers.

"Yeah, well, sorry. I was mad," says Kath. "'Cause you left me in the lurch. Or rather, in the lab."

"You were dead," I say.

"I was, but I changed my mind," she says. "I had something to live for. For the first time."

"What's that?" I say.

"Seriously?" Kath stops kicking at the door and looks at me.

"You and me?"

"You *said* it. You said you love me."

"I said it..." I don't know how to say it except to say it plainly. "...because you were dying."

It feels horrible. But it's the fairest thing I can find to say. I'm worried that this will hurt her feelings, but Kath doesn't seem particularly bothered.

"That's what you *thought*. That's what you tell yourself. The fact of the matter is, you don't know *what* you feel. But I do."

I shake my head. "Donna—"

"Is dead. Or as good as dead. You think you'll ever see her again? Look. Donna's a good kid. I *like* her. If I didn't, I'd have put a bullet in her a while ago. But you only *think* you love her because she's not around. You're after the unattainable. That's just a defense mechanism."

"What are you, a therapist?"

"I should be. I've been to enough of them," she says. She blows a strand of greasy blond hair from her eyes. "Personal, family, couples, you name it. And you are trying to keep yourself from getting intimately involved with me by pining after some chick who's thousands of miles from here. It's easier for you that way."

I consider it, a thought refracting through months and miles in the space of a heartbeat. Is it true? Am I just using the memory of Donna, a memory that morphs in the remembering, to keep myself away from the edge of Kath?

I remember how we met. An embrace on a subway platform. A night on the floor of the Metropolitan. A farewell at the lab as a tear of blood coursed from her eye.

Here in this back corridor, the sounds of the Uptowners trying to smash their way in have receded. Kath stands there, arms akimbo, hip jutting, her weight planted on one foot, radiating, as she always does, a beauty so blatant it's practically comical. There are definitely...feelings. And not just physical.

Maybe Donna really is gone for good. Maybe this weird jumble of emotions that Kath stirs up in me is something like love.

The last time I saw Donna, I was in the navy chopper, pulling away from the *Ronald Reagan*, our escape attempt botched. Donna lay on the flight deck looking up, getting smaller as a gout of flame spilled from the fuel hose she had just disconnected, saving the rest of us. I shouted her name, but the chop of the blades ate every other sound.

Donna wouldn't give up on me. I know it. She wouldn't just move on. She'd try to find her way back, or get me out of here.

"So?" says Kath. Only a moment has passed. We're still rummaging through the Apple Store, with no way out.

"So let's find a way out of here," I say. She frowns, turns to the door again, and kicks. The door gives way, and hardware spills out of the breach. Inside, a king's ransom in dead tech but no sign of a back door.

I go back to the front of the store and check in on Brainbox. He's awake, his eyes staring up at the ceiling. He mutters to himself, face waxy and slick with sweat. If we don't get him some help soon...

Then he looks at me and speaks. "Jefferson. Jefferson."

I lean down next to him.

"BB. I'm here. We're going to get you help."

He seems aware enough of our situation to look around weakly and laugh. It turns into a cough that feels like it'll rattle him to pieces. "Sure. But in the meanwhile. I have an idea."

BRAINBOX

THE WORLD IS DIMMING AND LOSING its purchase on the firmament resolving to liquid and disappearing through the hole in my stomach like the axis mundi they called it long ago the navel of the world the wormhole from heaven to earth I wonder if as I thought when I was a child when my eyes close for good the whole universe will simply disappear what a surprise it would be for everyone else to find out that they have only been tools and toys of my consciousness but no I realized long ago that the energy and computation required to maintain such an illusion just for me was more than any good efficient and parsimonious reason I could think of for it no the world will go on worlding and people will go on peopling and be about their business of lying cheating killing and stealing as ever and I will not be its experiencer but merely a pair of eyes shut on the monster with fourteen billion eyes but like a shark's teeth when one breaks another takes its place no if I want to make the

childhood daydream come true and wink out the world I must use
the biscuit and call forth the holy fire of the sun when they dropped
the first bomb it was even hotter than the sun right at the center
probably better to have been right there than half a mile away and
your skin sliding off your body and hanging like a burial shroud
that was the uranium bomb and they had a plutonium bomb and
they wanted to see how that would work so they dropped it three
days later before the enemy had a chance to surrender which would
have prevented the experiment conducted in righteous purpose
and turned it into an atrocity which of course it wasn't it was and
it was nothing stacked up against the babies I can summon with
the numbers in my head the A-bomb was a match compared to the
house fire I can start with the new warheads not to mention the dust
choking the atmosphere bringing winter forever I'll do it what does
all this mean to me when I'm gone why should I save them what did
they ever do for me but laugh and look sidelong only she only Chrysanthemum ever mattered a single damn and she's gone where well
who knows really she wasn't even she just a bunch of software on a
computer made of meat that thought it was a person and thought
it loved a person who was what I think is me really I have already
made the decision and just don't know it I have decided to kill them
all because it's time to move on and wipe creation's slate clean so
that maybe something better might come about but they've set
down the biscuit way over there a world away five feet away beyond
my reach and my graying flesh will not carry me that far so when

he appears from the back I say Jefferson I know a way to get help if you give me the biscuit he says why does he suspect that I'm going to do it no Jefferson likes to think the best of people he'd feel it'd be rude to accuse me of wanting to destroy the world but still he's concerned and so I tell him I can adjust the frequency of the device and send out a distress call whoever it was in those helicopters will receive it and come and he gets a light in his eye the way they always do when I figure something out for them and then I know I have him and he hands me the biscuit and I flip open its keypad cover but the device is dead and I could almost cry at the injustice of it the knife in my hand and the neck of the world beneath it but I cannot make the cut but then I remember where we are and I say get the batteries out of the laptops and bring me tools from the Genius Bar and the back room and they spring to action you can still hear the rattling of the gate as the Uptowners try to get at us I wonder are they clever enough to find the cargo entrance out back or are they just sniffing at their prey like dogs once I had a tribe and for a while I was beloved but only by Chrysanthemum not the rest they just loved the clean water and the working generators and who will they remember when they tell the story of the Cure not me no they will remember Jefferson though he was only the lab rat even he will die when I unleash the fire it is too bad but he had his chance to put it all back together and he failed Chrysanthemum when the nuke hits will my atoms drift with the wind to find yours in the Astor Court and in a million years can something come of the both of us no the

odds are against it there are really too many atoms it was much better when it was just a singularity if only I could take us back there
rewind time we would touch again but then I would lose you again
by unmeeting you and we would be unborn what a waste of energy it
all is but then what else does energy have to do than become matter
Jefferson hands me the batteries and the tools and I work at them as
they hold them gently ease a folded jacket behind my head look to
one another with sorrowful sorrow and I am suddenly engulfed by
a wave of sympathy and they are just poor witting creatures like me
oh my poor people what if I could have felt this connection before
why deny me it I look at their faces each suddenly dear will I kill
them all I must I must finish this fix it all the light comes on the
rubber tiles of the keypad illuminate and I begin there good-bye my
friends it is done it is accomplished

KATH

I WATCH THE FREAK, WHO HAS been MacGyvering the satellite phone with laptop batteries, wheezing and twitching with his mad scientist energy. Probably that's what's keeping him alive. Maybe he can make himself genuinely useful, fix one of these Macs and fire up an old download of the *Kardashians* or something. May as well pass the time before my old posse gets through the gate and the end comes.

Jefferson looks on, smiling and nodding and occasionally offering a low, practically hummed word of encouragement. He looks up from his perch by Brainbox's feet and smiles at him like everything's gonna be okay, the eternal optimist.

Maybe this is why I saved him from the crowd. They would have torn him to pieces, sooner or later.

Call it love if you like, but really it's a sort of addiction—and I've seen enough junkies to know. Or simply call it a need. I'd save a sandwich from danger if I was hungry. Which I am.

But starving would beat what's gonna happen if I fall into the hands of Uptown.

As if summoned, as if to say, *Think of the devil*, I hear his voice:

"Sis. Hey, Sis."

It's coming from under the gate. I look around—everyone else is nursing their wounds, preoccupied with their own shit. The twins are messing around with some ergonomic rubber-ball seat. Peter is lying under a table someplace feeling sorry for himself. Nobody to follow what's going on.

I don't say anything. I just creep toward the voice, trying to see if it can really be him.

"Sis," says Evan. "I know you're there."

It's him. I take the snub-nosed little Mauser from my belt. If I can figure out where he is, and I press the muzzle up close against the gate, maybe it will penetrate and get him.

"Sis, it hasn't been the same since you left," he says. "I miss you."

His voice sends me back to the breakfast table, long ago. A burble of traffic from twenty floors below, and Dad was using a newspaper to shield himself from human contact as he ate his paleo pancakes and rolled phone calls, murmuring to his assistant.

Evan looked up from his iPhone and saw the front page of the *New York Times*. I knew right away what he was looking at—an article about how the Islamic State was using captured women from some religious minority as sex slaves.

Evan asked for the newspaper, and Dad lowered it, looking at him.

"Since when do you read the paper?" asked Dad.

"I read it online," said Evan, which was bullshit. Evan never *read*; he *watched*, he *played*.

"Oh? Who's the vice president?" said Dad.

"Um, let me see… Oh, I remember. The vice president is Fuck You. Am I right?"

Now, usually Dad would have just hauled off and smacked Evan one across the teeth, but lately he'd been tailing off on the domestic violence, since Evan had been getting bigger. Instead, he'd begun cutting down on Evan's inheritance, like he was assessing penalty yards.

"That'll cost you another ten thousand, sport." He made a point of writing it down with his fountain pen on the creamy card-stock notepad he kept, bound in leather.

Evan wanted to say something back, escalate the contempt, but he didn't want to cost himself any more money, so he shut up. To reward his silence—silence had been, for years, what we kids bought things with—Dad gave him the paper when he was done. Call it behavioral conditioning.

Later, I saw Evan clip the sex slave article carefully, using one of his favorite knives to slit the edges. He put it in the file folder marked *cool shit* that he'd stolen from his internship at the hedge fund before he got shitcanned for selling coke to the analysts.

"Jerk-off material for those lonely nights?" I said.

"Go to hell, whore," he answered, always ready with a witty retort. Then, as though he hadn't just insulted me, he confided, "Hey, did you know you can tweet at the Islamic State dudes?"

"Are you insane?" I said. "The government will track you."

"I'm not using my real name, moron," he said. "I pretend I'm a seeker after truth, disillusioned with our materialistic way of life, thinking of converting to Islam. They *love* that shit."

"What the hell would you want to tweet terrorists for?"

"It's fucked up," he said, as if that were a good enough reason. "I mean, obviously we've got to eradicate them and shit. But they do have some good ideas."

And I thought, *I know the kind of ideas you like*. And again I repeated the magical, beautiful word to myself: *eighteen*. That's when the trust fund was going to kick in and I could get out, and the law and my parents and Evan couldn't stop me. And until then, I thought, please God keep Evan from getting the power to do what he wants.

Well, shit, God. Now you've done it. So I've decided to do something myself.

I say, "I'm here, Evan."

He sounds genuinely touched. "I knew it. I knew it. I knew you'd never leave me for good."

I can feel him near. I reach out the Mauser.

"Sis," he says, "listen to me. I've been doing a lot of thinking."

Probably not a record-breaking amount, I say to myself.

"Yeah?"

"Let's start again," he says. "I'm sorry for all the stuff I did. If you just open the gate, nobody's going to hurt you."

"Keep talking," I say. I want to get the aim right.

"Do you really want to do this?" he says. "Get hunted down like a rat, die in a hole with a bunch of losers? C'mon, open up. I can make you Queen of America."

I pull the trigger. *BAM!* The sound is deafening; my ears crackle with aftershock. As the others try to figure out what's happening, I pull the trigger again, unload the gun. Not even a bullet left for me.

Quiet and the smell of gunshots. Jefferson and Peter look up at me, astonished. Abel and Anna run over and cling to me.

Then through the metal gate comes his laughter. Bubbling up from the silence like swamp gas.

"Wow," he says. "I'll take that as a no, huh? Shit, you killed Mack. You remember him?"

I do.

"Couldn't happen to a nicer guy," I say.

"Well, Sis, now you really did it. You're gonna get the full treatment now. Don't say I didn't warn you."

And at that, I hear the *THUMP* of something igniting, and a tongue of brightness pokes through the gate.

"Shit," says Peter. "That's a welding torch."

The point of flame spits sparks onto the floor, where they dance around before dying.

Meanwhile, something is up with the freak.

"BB? BB?" says Jefferson, his voice unhinging. He's got the kid's face in his hands. I go over and look.

Kid's dead.

DONNA

LOOKY-LOOS KEEP PEEPING from the trees and the long grass, but they flee as the squaddies fire warning shots. I'm trying to talk Wakefield into cutting me loose from the handcuffs, when he turns to speak to Corporal Ayers.

Wakefield: "What have you got?"

Corporal Ayers: "It was on our frequency, sir. Just a short burst of Morse code." The way he says it makes it seem like that's extremely strange. Wakefield nods, and the squaddie continues.

Corporal Ayers: "It was a *terrible* fist, sir. All slurred innit. It's nothing but long and short bursts of static like. He's making the signal by interrupting the device's resting state. Like using static to communicate. It's actually rather clever."

Me: "What's a 'fist'?"

Corporal Ayers: "It's the way you do the Morse code signals, miss. Everybody's different. Dots and dashes longer or shorter than usual, spacing, that sort of thing."

Wakefield: "What's the message?"

Corporal Ayers: "I missed the first couple of signals, but what I've got is '11-AppleSt-FAO-WS.'"

Wakefield (turns to me): "I've never heard of an Apple Street. Have you?"

Me: "Oh, am I out of the doghouse?"

Wakefield: "Kindly answer."

Me: "There is no Apple Street. At least, not in Manhattan."

Wakefield: "Does any of the rest of it make sense to you?"

I look at Ayers, who consults his notepad and repeats the message. I turn the letters over in my mind. FAO. Then I know.

Me: "It's the Apple Store. FAO is FAO Schwarz. It was a toy store. There was an Apple Store near FAO Schwarz, like right down the street from it. It's *really* close, Colonel. We've got to go."

Wakefield: "Why do we have to go?"

My entire body is pounding.

Me: "Because it's my tribe. My friends. WS is Washington Square. And 11—it's the end of 911 and you didn't catch the beginning."

I can tell from Wakefield's face that he's hooked. But I doubt it's out of concern for my friends.

Titch: "That frequency is only military."

Wakefield looks up at him and nods. "Could be it."

I think he means the signal has to have been sent from the biscuit.

Me, I know the only member of our tribe who'd be likely to know Morse code. And he happens to be the guy smart enough to figure out how to send a radio message using a doomsday device.

Brainbox is calling. Which means so is Jefferson.

KATH

JEFFERSON CRADLES HIM LIKE A BABY, tears running down his face. I sure hope he got this worked up when *I* died.

Brainbox's eyes are closed. But he doesn't look like he's asleep. He looks like he's an *it*. A corpse.

Whatever was inside is gone and it isn't coming back, so this is no time to get sentimental.

"Jeff," I say. "I know you feel bad, but we've got to figure something out, like, now. They're cutting their way in."

Before he can respond, the biscuit starts beeping. I kneel down and pick it up. There's a shitty little screen, like on an old calculator from the seventies or something, and it reads COMMAND INITIATED.

Uh-oh.

"Uh, Jeff?" I say. "I think whatshisface might've just started World War Three."

Jefferson glares at me. "He wouldn't do that. You're crazy."

"Crazy is as crazy does," I say. I feel like I'm a better judge than most. And frankly, not to throw shade on the dead and whatnot, but the kid always struck me as two sandwiches short of a picnic— especially after his waify little girlfriend got her ticket punched by that polar bear. I would absolutely not put it past him to torch the world in, like, the ultimate mad scientist mic drop.

And Jefferson feels it, too. He doesn't want to say so, I can tell, but in his mind's eye I bet he's seeing the missiles launch, starting the long loops toward Moscow and Beijing.

As if on cue, we hear a combustible whooshing.

But it's not the bombs flying overhead. It's the sound of the arc welder as the gate is finally breached, a semicircle of pleated metal crashing to the floor, leaving a giant mouse hole. The welding flame sucks up the open air, hissing with satisfaction.

I have to laugh, because what's the worst that can happen? No matter how bad things get, the end is near; I figure we have maybe a half hour before the Russians return fire and their nukes dip back into the atmosphere to fry New York.

As the Uptowners start to push in, the twins get to it, cracking heads, but they're soon tackled. I see Peter swarmed by a couple of camouflaged bros, and then Jefferson gets up and holds my hand. In his other, a pistol.

I kiss him, hard. He kisses back. Then I look at the gun. "End it," I say.

Jefferson puts the pistol to my head. And I figure, why not? Why not by his hand? I laugh, because we could have saved a lot of time if he had just killed me the first time we met, on the subway platform.

I look into his eyes. Let it come.

Suddenly, we hear a hullabaloo from outside—"Look! Holy shit!"—and Jefferson lowers the gun. I figure, *Ah, somebody's seen the white tails of our ICBMs off to do their business of eliminating humanity.*

But that's not it, either. I hear an English accent, amplified.

"Attention. Vacate the area immediately, or we will fire. Vacate the area."

I have no time to figure this out before Evan appears in front of us, smiling. There's another guy with him, whose name must be Chapel, because that's what Jefferson shouts—

—at just about the same time that Evan clocks me with a right cross and I tumble backward.

It's not the first time he's hit me, but it's one of the hardest, and I feel the cotton wool filling up my brain as I taste blood in my mouth.

The rest is a little hazy. I hear some shots and then the *brrrrap* of some kind of gun that I'm not familiar with. Kids are falling and running and screaming, and then the store fills with smoke pouring out of a little black canister.

An Uptowner dude stands over me and raises a big aluminum bat. And, in the old slowing-down-of-time thing that would appear, actually, to be what happens before you die, I can read the brand, Mikasa, in angular blue lettering along the side as it hangs in the air...

But before he's got a chance to bludgeon me, a strange little guy appears out of the smoke, brandishing a kind of curvy machete thing, and chops the dude's hand off. The bat clangs on the ground with the disembodied fist still gripping the handle.

Well, that's odd.

The Uptowner dude is screaming about his hand until another, much bigger guy—like, professional-wrestling size—steps up and bashes him in the face, and he goes unconscious.

"You awright, miss?" the big guy asks.

Now the thing about this guy? He's not just big. He's *old*. Like, thirty years old.

"Where is it?" says the voice I heard over the loudspeaker, only this time it's coming from the source, a square-jawed English guy in what, judging from the gray blocky print, appears to be urban-warfare camo.

Then I guess I start hallucinating, because who should I see but Donna, same shitty haircut but with a few extra pounds. Like, not quite as teenage boyish as before. Like she's been living it up someplace.

She's got a bunch of soldiers with her, some of whom are little sparkpluggy guys with sickles, like the one who just saved my bacon. The other half are more big, pasty white dudes.

Lastly, there's a copper-skinned guy with a less military air than the rest. Jeez, I thought *I* was pretty. Dude is hot.

At about this point, the events of the past few weeks—bushwhacking my way back from the island, escaping from the UN, going to ground in Midtown, trying to murder my brother—start to take their toll on me. I'm not usually the fainting type, but can you blame me? Days of ditch water and expired protein bars. Fortunately, I get that swimmy feeling before it happens, so I have a moment before the dissolve sets in. Quick, think of something pithy.

"Welcome to New York," I say, and crumble.

DONNA

JUST BEFORE MY OLD FRIENTAGONIST Kath collapses onto the floor, Rab, never missing a chance to be swoony, makes a grab for her and lowers her down gently. Jefferson also looks like he's about to fall over, but I'm not sure Rab is going to rush to his aid, so I take it upon myself. He falls into my arms—not in a Harlequin romance sort of way, more in a ton of bricks sort of way. I practically throw out my back holding him up. It wasn't quite what I had in mind—I was envisioning more of a wind-machine, Rihanna video kind of thing. Still. It feels like every cell in my body is suddenly flooded with warmth, as though each little mitochondrion suddenly got a case of the feels. I burrow my cheek into the crook of his neck, breathe him in.

I help Jeff over to one of the weirdly preserved wooden display tables in the store.

Jefferson: "You're here."

Me: "Yes."

I had been figuring our reunion would be a little more roman-tic, like I'd say, *I've traveled across oceans of time and defied death to find you,* or something, and he'd say, *I knew my love would draw you back to me,* or something, but in the moment "You're here" and "Yes" just about covers it. Anyhow, we've played this scene before. There's nothing worth saying that you don't already know. Just our being here is enough. Besides, there is one teeny-tiny pressing issue.

Me: "Do you have it, Jeff? The biscuit."

Jefferson: "Brainbox."

Something about the way he says it . . .

Reza, the squad medic, is over by BB. He performs a few last chest compressions, seemingly for my benefit. Or you could look at it as a ritual, to appease the god of his craft.

I hear a last gust of air escape, a ghostly wheeze, but I know that it's the breath that Reza just forced into him.

I sit down next to Brainbox and take his hand. It's cold as clay.

Go to SeeThrough, I say in my head.

The squaddies confer with Wakefield. Sounds like the biscuit is no place to be found.

Wakefield: "It's time to go, Miss Zimmerman."

Me: "We take him, too." I mean Brainbox.

Wakefield: "I understand why you're saying that, but—"

Me: "If he doesn't go, I don't."

Wakefield looks to Guja, clearly calculating the cost/benefit of hog-tying me as opposed to carrying Brainbox out with us.

Wakefield: "Take the body, Sergeant."

PETER

THERE'S A MOMENT, AFTER THE BRITS and the little guys have arrived, when I have a bead on him. I'm on my back, but I pull myself up and hold out the pistol. And there, over the gun sight, I see Chapel prying the biscuit from Brainbox's hands.

He looks up and sees me but says nothing—or if he does say anything, it's whirled up in the echoes and screams and reports around us.

And I can't pull the trigger.

Why? Not because I love him. I hate him just as much.

Can it be because I'm still hoping we'll get back together? Pathetic. Maybe if I had time to think rationally, I *would* shoot him. But in a moment, I lose him in the traffic of bodies, and then the chance is gone.

I just lie back down, letting the party go on for a little bit without me. The twins rouse themselves and help Kath back into consciousness. Soldiers search the store. Jeff and Donna sit by Brainbox's body, crying.

Later, when I have gathered up a few shards of my self-respect, I sidle up to Donna.

"It's been like *forever*, girl. How you been?" I say it like we've been on different vacations or something.

Donna laughs. It's a charity laugh. "You know, this and that." She takes a breath. "Are we gonna talk about Brainbox?"

"Not yet." She understands. We do this. Put it aside, let it cool down. And speaking of cooling down... "Who's the hot guy?"

"Oh, *him*," she says. "That's Rab."

"Hmm." I look at her face. "How long you been hitting that?"

She stares daggers. She knifes me with her eyes. "Sonofabitch. Don't tell Jefferson."

"*Girrrl...*" This is some juicy stuff.

"I mean, I'm going to tell him myself. Anyway, that's over. It was a mistake."

"If *that's* a mistake, I'd love to see you get it right."

So Donna fills me in on the last few months: imprisonment, transport to England, a new identity, a few months at this fancy-pants university, all the time getting pumped for information by the Brits. It sounds all tragic the way she tells it, but I'm like, I wish *I* coulda been seduced and betrayed if it's like *that*.

I tell her about the trip from the island back to Manhattan, Brainbox building a bomb out of pigeon poop gathered by yours truly, retaking Washington Square from the Uptowners, the Gathering at the UN, and, finally, Chapel.

"I'm really sorry, Petra."

"I thought he was the one."

"Maybe there isn't a *one*," says Donna. "Maybe you get to decide."

"Yeah, I don't really have much time to date at the moment. And not *everybody* meets a soul mate every two minutes." I look at Rab, who is looking over at us, trying, I guess, to figure out what Donna is saying about him.

"Shut up." Then, "I really am sorry about Chapel. Not just for the, you know, geopolitical consequences."

I want to say something like *It's okay*, but it isn't. Nothing is okay about that. It's pretty much the opposite of okay. It's *yako*.

"He used me, Donna," I say.

"I know them feels," she says.

I should have shot him. But I couldn't. Maybe it was that lingering sense of love and affection that, for all its outrageousness, I can still somehow hear over the crazy-making tinnitus of heartbreak and anger. I'm not proud of myself. Chapel killed Brainbox. And I hate him for it. But some part of my brain is still running his app in the background, figuring *somehow* we might work it all out. And naturally, the first and most vital step in that sequence was my demurring vis-à-vis blowing his brains out.

Surely that counted for something? My doing him a solid like that?

Outside the store, it's like a video game kill screen, with bodies splayed this way and that, looking that uncool narcoleptic way they do. The British invasion went all *Downton Abbey* on these fools, and the Uptowners didn't take a one of 'em along to the big sleep. I feel like it'd be a different story if the fighting weren't all in the open like this. In the catacombs of the Bazaar, or the mazes of SoHo, the Brits would lose the advantage. But here, the soldiers cleaned house.

One of the gherkins—I think that's what Donna called them—hefts poor Brainbox in a fireman's carry, and we hustle behind him in a parade to Central Park. It seems quiet on the street, but I know that the Uptowners are watching, peeping from their high windows, figuring what to do. Homeboys don't take defeat lightly.

About half a mile into the park, there's a little encampment around two nasty-looking black helicopters. We stop within a rough circle that's been hacked into the high grass. A few gherkins are expanding the circle, whacking away with their crazy elbowed knives. The guy in charge, Wakefield, tells them to stop and get ready to move out.

"Not yet. We're burying our friend," says Donna.

"No time for that," says Wakefield.

"So shoot me," says Donna.

Wakefield looks like he's thinking about it.

"Have a heart," says the Cracker Shaq, who seems to have a soft spot for Donna.

Wakefield thinks, says, "I need to debrief the..." He's about to say *prisoners*, I think, but he stops himself and says "contacts."

It's a standoff until I say, "Don't worry. I'll talk. You start with Brainbox, Donna."

That seems to be a fair compromise, so Jefferson and Donna and the huge guy carry Brainbox over a ways and I stay with the troops.

I'm clearing off some snow from beneath a tree when the Beautiful Bronze One steps up to me.

"Hello," he says. "My name is Rab. You'll be Peter."

Yes I will. I offer him a seat next to me, out of the wind.

"Hi, Rab. You gonna take my briefs off?"

"It's 'debrief,' but I think you know that," he says.

To be honest, I thought this would throw him, like, the full-on Nelly. I wanted to see how he'd react. He's smiling. A natural flirt, happy to roll both ways up to a certain point, at least that's what my gaydar, autobooting out of dormancy, tells me.

I read about this a long time back, when there was this thing called the Internet. Some of these high-class British boys are that way. Like, it's traditional to be a little gay for each other in boarding school, and then later, when you're a captain of industry or whatever, you conveniently forget about it.

And a guy like this would've had *opportunities*. But it's strange; he doesn't seem like Donna's type. Then again, when you're *that* good-looking, you're kind of like O-negative blood—universal. I would definitely swipe right on the brother, if you know what I mean.

Okay, *actually*, I've only got eyes for Chapel. I mean I know I'm a guy and all? Like with a broken sex-drive override switch? But I already did the thing where you make up for hurt with sex, what seems like long ago. For now, I'm happy to play the dizzy lovestruck queen with Rab, if it'll give me an angle on what's going down.

This is all about the football, of course. The biscuit. The button. The bomb. That's what they came for, even if they're pretending to give a shit about the Cure and all of us imperiled young'uns. *They* being the Brits plus the various lucky and/or rich folks who made it out of the US, backed up by our navy, which more or less runs this bitch vis-à-vis world trade. *They* could give two shits about us apocalescents. That much I *do* believe about what Chapel said.

What they *can* spare some feces for is the Doomsday Car Phone, which was moments ago snatched out of Brainbox's hands and out of their reach by Chapel and the nastiest bunch of white boys you'd ever want to run screaming from. Seeing Chapel with the Uptowners is pretty much the worst possible version of when your ex starts running with a new crowd.

I give Rab more or less the straight scoop, neglecting to mention the fact that Brainbox had the launch codes memorized. Brother's dead, why go into it—besides, if they knew that, they'd probably wonder if he had time to write them down. Which he did, or at least, I wrote them down for him. Brother was going in and out of consciousness, though, so who knows how reliable his memory was at that point. I wasn't about to double-check it on the biscuit, know what I'm saying? I may be a troublemaker on occasion, but I'm not down to start World War III.

Be that as it may, I don't tell Rab about the folded piece of paper in my back pocket with all those strings of letters.

Chapel has the biscuit now, of course, which means that my ex is the most dangerous man on the planet. Funny thing is, that sort of makes it worse. I know there should be some point where the jealousy kind of shorts out in the face of this evil that is obviously much bigger than just breaking up with me.

But it's more like if somebody I dated was suddenly starring in a big movie that everybody wanted to go see. Yeah, it makes it hella worse that he's moved on to bigger and better things like blowing up the planet.

Least, I guess that's what he might do. Or maybe Chapel wants to use the threat of the bombs to change things, like bring down the government or make things more equal or stuff. Back in the day, when he was recruiting us to help the Resistance, he was all about—if memory serves—"redressing injustice and shattering the hold of the oligarchy on the levers of power" and whatnot. Maybe he really wants to make the world a better place.

Or maybe he just wants to launch everything, fuck things up for real, and clean the slate.

Who knows? One way or another, he shouldn't have done me like that.

The truth? Just between you and me? Part of me doesn't even care. I don't care about the nukes and I don't care about the politics. All I care is that he's gone and he doesn't want me. But whatever he *does* want, he is definitely holding a big stick.

DONNA

TITCH MAKES SHORT WORK OF digging the grave, heaving the cold-hardened soil out of the ground in massive clumps. The guy is a beast.

He never met Brainbox, of course, but he knows about him, on account of he must have read my interrogation transcripts. Titch might look like Shrek, all bulk and muscle, but he's smart and he's thorough. I reckon (as my Cambridge buddies would say) he's helping me because he knows Brainbox was one of my tribe, and he still feels guilty toward me for knowing about the whole honeypot scam with Rab. Besides, he understands that BB cured the Sickness, pretty much. We're burying a hero. But he won't get a monument. He'll get a bald patch in Sheep Meadow.

Me: "Titch." He looks up at me from the hole.

Titch: "Miss."

Me: "Can you tell me something?" He just looks back at me. "The guy who got the biscuit, Chapel. He said the Reconstruction Committee doesn't care about us. I mean us 'kids,' or whatever you want to call us. He said that you just wanted what was left after you let us all die."

Titch opens his mouth to say something, but then he thinks better of it. He leans the spade against the side of the grave.

Titch: "I think I dug deep enough, miss," he says finally. Then he levers himself out of the ground and shuffles off, leaving us "to say words."

Jefferson and I finish cleaning Brainbox off with surgical wipes. Jeff jumps into the hole, and I help lower in the body. It's so easy that it's hard—I mean, like, emotionally speaking. Brainbox is touchingly light. The guy forgot to eat at the best of times. When he was working on a problem, he might go days without a meal.

I stretch my hand down to Jefferson to help him out of the ground. I have to lean back, practically fall, to keep from getting pulled in, and as he steps over the lip of the grave, we crumple into a ball together. It should be intimate; after everything I've gone through to get back to him, it should feel like home. But instead, it's awkward. There's a distance that we can't seem to span—not yet at least. Maybe he smells another guy on me. I don't know.

We stand there looking at Brainbox below the ground as

flies land and start to test the waters of his flesh. I want to figure out something to say, something that would make a difference if Brainbox were listening. He would've insisted it was pointless, though; he said that consciousness ended at death, so there's nobody left to care about how you treat them or what you say.

Jefferson doesn't seem to be coming up with anything, either. We've said it all before, over other bodies of other friends. Jefferson's brother, Wash. Half our tribe.

So we just stand there for a while.

I want to think about Brainbox, give him his due. But my mind keeps returning to Titch's non-answer.

It'd be nice if what Rab said was true. He says his job is to make contact with the Relevant Authorities—which is optimistic, both the idea that there *are* authorities and that, if there were, we could make contact with them—and begin the process of "reintegration." The lost boys and girls of New York and the rest of the plague-ridden continent will be taken under the wing of the Reconstruction Committee.

But I don't buy it. Rab, I suspect, is here as my handler, The Powers That Be figuring that I still have feelings for him, which is *so* not true.

And if this were a diplomatic mission, I'd say we're a little heavy on firepower. It's pretty obvious to me that the point of this little jaunt is to find the biscuit so that the fate of the world doesn't end up in the hands of a bunch of juvenile delinquents. Maybe if it weren't for that, they'd have preferred, as Chapel nicely put it, to wait until everybody was dead and then scrape up the goo.

From the way Wakefield is giving clipped orders to the squaddies and the Gurkhas, I can tell he's burning up because we were so close to getting ahold of the biscuit. And I can't say that I'm 100 percent stoked that Chapel and Evan have it, either. A revolutionary and a sadist don't add up to a great decision-making process, I figure.

Wakefield looks over at us, calculating how long he can let this sad little excuse for a funeral go before he can get on the move. I figure this gesture at propriety may be the last chance Jefferson and I have to speak privately for a while.

Me: "They came for the biscuit, Jefferson."

Jefferson: "I know." He looks away from me, over the bone-white expanse of the meadow. He says, "What did you come for?"

Me: "Do you have to ask?"

Jefferson: "I thought . . . I didn't want to assume anything."

Is this the same Jefferson? The boy who made a little home with me in a metal corner of the carrier? Who declared his undying

77

love for me in the Reading Room, with the coffered paintings of heaven above us?

No. He's older. He's defeated. I can tell that much from his face, and from what Peter said. Jefferson's dream of Utopia is done. He's a hunted man. So it bears saying.

Me: "Jeff. I came for you."

I want that to be enough to change the look in his eyes; it isn't. What's happened?

I ask him something I've neglected to until now.

Me: "The tribe. What happened to the rest of us?"

He takes a while to answer, a strange look on his face.

Jefferson: "Washington Square is gone, Donna. I don't know where most of the tribe went. Holly, Elena, and Ayesha were still alive when the Gathering started, at least."

Me: *"Gathering?"*

Jefferson: "I tried to get all the tribes together. I—we—wanted to make a united front, before the grown-ups arrived."

This is Jefferson, all right. Always trying to fix the world.

Jefferson: "We almost did it. Then Theo and Kath showed up and told everybody that there were places where the Sickness hadn't hit."

Me: "Wait—what? *You* didn't tell them?"

Jefferson: "I was going to. We just needed a little time. We needed to get the new constitution *first*."

78

I'm trying to weigh that in my mind, but I still want to know about the others.

Me: "And everybody else from the Square?"

Jefferson: "A lot of the boys are dead. And the Uptowners have the girls, the ones they didn't kill…"

Jefferson looks off, and I realize what the strange expression on his face is. It's shame. Our breath billows out like steam in the freezing air. Wakefield hovers nearby, clearly waiting for a moment to break up the funeral.

Me: "What do you mean, the Uptowners *have* them?"

Jefferson: "They took them away, before we even got back to the Square. They'd taken the place over. Brainbox made a bomb… We brought down one of the buildings on the north side. Killed some of the Uptowners. But the girls were gone." He scrapes away at the snow with his foot, uncovering the dark, wet grime below. I can hear the twins screaming and laughing as they toss snowballs at each other, and Kath, amusingly enough, tells them no aiming for the head.

Me: "Took them *where*?"

Jefferson turns, looks around, as if he might see our missing girls somewhere by chance. Nothing but the squaddies gearing up.

Jefferson: "I don't know. The Bazaar, maybe. I don't know."

Me: "This 'Gathering' of yours—were the Uptowners there?"

Jefferson won't meet my eyes. I'm dreading the answer. If he actually *worked* with them, *compromised* with them...

Then he looks me in the eye.

Jefferson: "Yes."

My heart sinks. It goes down about a thousand feet underwater, where you have to wear a special suit to keep from imploding.

Me: "And you...you *knew* that they had our people?" No answer. Which means yes. "Jefferson...you didn't try to get them back?"

Jefferson: "I was going to."

Me: *"When?"*

Jefferson: "Once the doc was signed. The constitution. That needed to come first. We needed to have the Uptowners be part of it, Donna. Or the whole thing wouldn't work."

Me: "So you just—what—hung around with those...*monsters*, while our people were somewhere getting...with God knows what happening to them?"

Jefferson: "I *had* to. I had to deal with them. For everyone's sake."

I think of what the Uptowners stand for and what they do to girls. The pimps and prostitutes at the Bazaar. The things that happened to Kath that she won't even talk about. I think of the Mole People, literally forced underground because they wouldn't submit to them. And *now* I know what I *really* came here for.

I take his hands. Our breath mingles in the cold air.

Me: "Okay. Jefferson. I guess I did come for you. For your sake. You want to get out from under this? Redeem yourself? Then you listen to me. You can forget about the big picture for a little while." I speak to him gently, but I don't leave any room for doubt or questions. "Stop dreaming. Think about our *friends*. You and me, we are going to find them. If we do one thing, if we die doing it, we are going to get those girls back from Uptown. You understand?"

Jefferson: "The nukes—"

Me: "Will have to wait. First we save our family. *Then* we save the world."

Rab: "It's the same thing, isn't it?"

It's now that I realize Rab is standing nearby, peering down curiously into Brainbox's grave, close enough to have heard everything. He doesn't appear to have snuck up or anything. He's just standing there with his usual air of Cool Guy confidence, like he can talk his way into any party or any conversation.

Rab: "Why choose between nuclear blackmail and white slavery?" He's bright and upbeat. "Our quarry is Chapel and his pet psychotic, right? Find them and we find your girls, don't we?"

Kath: "No. We don't." She's sauntered over from the snowball fight.

Great. Now everybody is joining in. The sacred mood broken,

Titch circles around us and starts filling in Brainbox's grave, clearly hurrying things along.

Kath continues, "If your girls have been taken, they'll be at the museum."

Me: "What museum?"

Kath: "The one with the dinosaurs. That's where the slave market is."

Jefferson: "The Museum of Natural History. On Central Park West. That's, like, half a mile from here."

Kath: "They take them there to make them into Fun Girls." Off my look, she explains, "Slaves. There's these creepy West Side religious nuts who do it. They keep them there for a while, break them down. Then they sell them."

Me: "Then that's where I'm going."

Wakefield comes over, seeing that the memorial service is busting up.

Wakefield: "It's time to get going. We should hit Grand Central in an hour."

Titch looks back at Wakefield but leaves me to explain.

Me: "Change in plans, Colonel. We've got to rescue some of our friends first."

Wakefield: "Those aren't my orders."

Me: "*I* don't have any orders."

Wakefield: "You are under my protection."

Me: "I don't need your protection."

Wakefield: "You are under my *supervision*."

Me: "We could use more hands if we're going to fight the Uptowners."

Wakefield: "I don't think you're qualified to speak on military issues."

Which I guess *technically* is correct? But practically? We sort of *do* know what we're talking about. Which is to say, we've slugged our way through two years of chaos here, against everything the place could throw at us—cannibals, fascists, even tweens.

Me: "I'm sorry, but my decision stands. You can help, or wait here for me, or go do your thing."

Titch: "That wasn't the plan, miss."

Me: "So? You've been here, what, half a day? You think any kind of plan *lasts* here? This place has its own rules. So I'm making my own plans from now on. I know that you've got to do what you've got to do. That's okay. You don't have to watch my back anymore, Titch." I turn to Kath and Peter and Jefferson. "You want to come along, that's up to you."

I stand there hoping, as people decide. It's kinda like in the Lord of the Rings? When one group goes to Mordor and the other goes to that big castle place. It's like everybody has to decide: Will it be A plot or B plot? And which one is the A plot? Well, maybe I can be excused for thinking it's *me*, even if it doesn't involve saving the world from destruction. So who else is coming?

Maybe, just maybe I care more about what Jefferson is going to do than anybody else. And maybe his decision is really about whether we'll have a future together. And maybe, even though I know he is all about the Big Picture, I want him to be about the small picture, which is actually, in fact, the big picture as far as everyone we might actually help is concerned.

Jefferson: "I'm with you." He reaches out his hand, touches mine lightly.

Maybe that matters a lot.

Kath: "Me too, I guess. I think you can take it as a given that these little creeps are along for the ride." She gestures at the Thrill Kill Twins, who practically wag their tails.

The Gurkha takes a step toward me.

Guja: "Wakefield said you stay with us." His hand reaches for his knife, the locus of his authority. But then he finds Titch's giant mitt resting on his shoulder.

Titch: "I don't think so, Guja. I reckon this is her call."

Guja looks to Wakefield, who suddenly seems thwarted. I'm not too sure about the command structure here. Maybe I thought Wakefield was the guy in charge because Titch is ginormous and working-class and Wakefield is human-size and fancy. But Titch is working for the Reconstruction Committee, at least for the spy guys who work with them. I guess Wakefield is just regular army.

Wakefield: "There's no question of delaying. And we need a local guide. That's why they're here in the first place."

Then, a surprise.

Peter: "I'll stay with you, Colonel." Instead of meeting my eyes, he looks at his shoes, which frankly aren't much to look at, bedraggled navy-issue sneakers covered in filth.

Me: "Really?"

He finally looks back up.

Peter: "He's right. They're gonna need a guide. Besides, I have to. You understand?"

At first, no. But then it makes sense after a second. He means he has to deal with Chapel.

Me: "Petra—"

Peter: "No advice, please. No tough love. I know. He was using me. I know there's nothing to be said. But . . . Look. He fooled me. He fooled all of us. Right? Well, somebody has to hold him to account. If not, and that fool Evan becomes, like, some kind of supervillain, I'll never be able to live with myself."

Damn it, I'm crying again, in front of these old-world tough guys and the people I'm supposed to lead into battle. But the feels don't care, my eyes don't care. Come to think of it, I don't care. Too much has happened for it to matter whether it's good management style.

And there's good reason to cry. Maybe I won't ever see Petra again. In this place, you say good-bye to somebody, it's just as likely it'll be forever.

Wakefield is satisfied with the deal. Maybe he's relieved to be rid of me. I hug Peter a long time. Then I turn to go. But there's another surprise to come.

Rab: "I'm coming with you."

Oh, no he didn't.

Me: "This isn't your problem." Besides which, I'm not sure I actually want him along. The mission is challenging enough without balancing a love triangle on my shoulders. Plus, I hate him. Right?

Rab's eyes narrow. Calculating.

Rab: "We made an investment in you. I'm just keeping an eye on it." But he says it in a way that makes it seem like he hardly means it. Like he's speaking for the benefit of Titch and Wakefield, not for me. "Besides, we need to keep our communications open. I'll stay in contact with Titch over our comms. We'll rendezvous after we help your friends."

Rab looks over at Titch, who nods.

Titch: "Keep an eye on her." He says it like, *Make sure she doesn't do anything wrong,* but I know—or I feel—that he means *Protect her,* since he can't.

Titch holds out his hand, big as a kid's baseball glove. I go up on tiptoes and kiss him on the cheek.

Me: "Keep your head down, you big lug."

Titch: "Stay safe, miss."

I turn to Peter and say, "I'll be seeing all of you soon." But I know that's probably a lie.

We stalk westward through tall grass browned by the frost. The snow swallows our footfalls. It's remarkably peaceful here, nothing but a corpse or two observing our progress.

That is, until we encounter a bunch of randoms hauling ass our way, scared out of their minds. I waylay one of them—a firearm helps in getting people to stop and chat—and ask what's gotten into her.

Random chick: "Oldies. From outside. Majorly strapped."

I figure she must mean the rest of the British squad.

Me: "How many?"

Random chick: "I don't know. Twenty, thirty? You'll see for yourself soon enough. They're coming this way."

I turn to Rab.

Me to Rab: "Was there another team? More squaddies?"

Rab: "Not that I know of." He takes in my look. "I'm telling you the truth. I have no idea who they are."

Ahead of us is a redbrick compound, still within the walls of the park. There's a forecourt with upturned tables, and then inside, we find a restaurant called Tavern on the Green, its shiny wood and green carpets all beat to shit. We wait by the windows, eyes peeled, ears cored.

Five minutes on, I hear the crunching of broken glass under rubber-soled boots, like some giant beast chewing a barrel of Grape-Nuts. I peek through what's left of a broken window, to see a squad of soldiers walking down the tarmac path that leads past the restaurant toward the west end of Sheep Meadow. Over the jagged edges of the glass, I can see a flutter of camouflage. To my now-connoisseurial eye, it looks different from both the British regulation and the Uptowners' store-bought dress-up stuff.

Someone delivers a gruff, monosyllabic command, and the crunching stops. Now I can see, in the reflections of a bent piece of chrome-plated window frame, some soldiers close by in gray-green camouflage and sloped helmets, faces obscured by ski masks. They carry long, pipe-barreled rifles I don't recognize.

I look over at Rab. He shakes his head. *No idea.*

Then the soldiers start talking, and it has the rolling, rhotic, diphthong-heavy sound of Russian. They're muttering to one another in low tones, guarded, suspicious of something, but I hear the words *Central Park* (or rather, *Tsintril Pyark*) pop out of the flow. I see a soldier straighten the folds of a map. Then something stops their talk. A hushed order, and the soldiers scatter.

I realize, to my horror, that at least one of them has made a beeline for the building and is right on the other side of the short outer wall of the restaurant's façade, so there's maybe eight inches of brick between us and some kind of Russian supersoldier. I can hear his breathing, slow and measured; I can see the nub of his rifle barrel poking over the ledge of the window frame. I look back at the others, crouching frozen on the floor by some nearby banquettes.

They haven't noticed us yet, but now we're effectively pinned, and if the Russians decide to look inside, they'll have us dead to rights. A copper penny of fear forms on my tongue.

I try to stay silent and look for something to concentrate on to stop from trembling. Across the floor, an abandoned plastic doll stares at me with glassy blue eyes. She's naked and sexless, arms reaching upward like she's begging or celebrating.

Then I spot Jefferson, reaching out for the doll. He swivels her arms back to a less awkward pose and sets her on a soft cushion away from the broken glass. He's always had a weird thing about stuffed animals and such being left in uncomfortable positions, and, yeah, I can see how holding her arms up like that must've been really tiring for her nonexistent plastic back muscles. He looks up and sees me seeing him and blushes.

There's a sound from the path, and I see gray-green movements reflected in the pupils of Jefferson's eyes. Then I look up to find a young soldier staring down at me, his gun poised lightly in his hands. He has a look of consternation on his face.

I put my hands up, and the others do, too. There doesn't seem to be much else for it. Then we hear a *CRACK* in the distance, and our Russian soldier falls forward into the restaurant, bleeding from the neck. He's practically on top of me.

There's a chorus of pops and bangs as the Russians fire back at whoever was stupid enough to engage. Meanwhile, the wounded soldier is scrabbling at his collar. Then his crazed eyes light on me and oscillate quickly between fear and hope.

It's pretty unlikely that this guy is gonna be around long. There's just so much important wiring in too little real estate in the neck. You've got your trachea, your esophagus, your carotid and cervical arteries… But what am I supposed to do, just let him croak? He's got nothing to do with Uptown or Washington Square or any of this—he may as well be E.T.

I bend over him and put pressure on the wound. It's a pretty neat little hole, and my guess is his spine is still intact, considering he's still moving his extremities. I shift my hand away from the hole for a peek and, amazingly, spot a nub of metal, the edge of a bullet, resting against the blue-purple sheath of his carotid artery. It didn't hit him at full velocity—might have been a ricochet. I can see it's no less painful for all that, though; the bullet twists slightly as he struggles.

It's difficult to concentrate in the thunderstorm of gunfire just outside. But it seems to me that while the guy has lucked out in terms of wound location, the jagged little slug will nick the carotid at any moment if I don't get it out.

He's not going to thank me for it, though.

I look over in the general direction of Jefferson.

Me: "Help me hold this guy down!"

Jefferson crawls over, nearly bumping into Rab, who's coming over as well. After a momentary mutual glare, each of them grabs one of the soldier's arms and holds the poor guy steady.

Since I don't have my old wound kit—they took it from me what feels like centuries ago, at the lab—I take a deep breath and carefully poke the ends of my fingers into the blood-slick wound. A muffled scream. My fingertips feel around for purchase on the slug, which turns suddenly elusive. It tucks back into the tortured flesh like a frightened mouse. I overcome my revulsion and my pity for the soldier and squeeze my fingers further, until finally, I grab hold of the bullet and pluck it out.

Tears roll from the soldier's eyes, and he looks at me with baffled incomprehension. I take his hand and press it to the wound.

Me: "Don't let go."

I fish around in my bag and come up with a precious roll of duct tape I stole from the helicopter. I swab at the wound with the top of his shirt, then rip off a square of silvery tape and slap it down over the hole.

Some notion of what's happened is now lighting up the guy's

eyes when suddenly he's pulled over the threshold by his legs, which have all the time been crooked over the edge of the window frame.

Amazingly, in the chaos of the firefight, the rest of the Russians don't seem to notice us. They'll be hella surprised when they find my ghetto bandage.

The wounded soldier's eyes linger one last moment in the window hole before he disappears, carried away to wherever the Russians are retreating. The sound of gunfire dies down. We're left in stunned and bruised silence.

PETER

WE DOUBLE-TIME IT BACK THROUGH SHERIDAN Square, past the golden dude on the golden horse, whoever he is, past the Plaza Hotel. The Gurkhas and the buzz-cut troops leapfrog ahead of one another and scamper from one piece of architecture to the next so that, if you looked at it from above, we could be a big superorganism slithering amorphously along. It all seems very convincing and *Call of Duty* and whatnot.

Still, I know we shouldn't be out here in the street. After our little tussle at the Apple Store, the Uptowners will be on alert. I catch up with Wakefield as he strides down Forty-First and make the argument.

"I appreciate your opinion," he says, even though he obviously doesn't. "But we're perfectly capable of traveling half a mile on foot quickly and safely."

"And I, like, appreciate *your* opinion? But you've got to recognize it *won't* be quick and safe if you try to just sashay over to Grand Central."

Now here's the thing. I wish I could present my ideas better at this moment. Because I'm *right,* but when Wakefield looks at me, all he sees is a gay seventeen-year-old n-word. And that doesn't cut much ice in his world. I can tell that he has about zero time for my advice.

"If our first encounter was any measure of their capabilities—"

"It wasn't," I say, interrupting him, which I guess he's not used to. "The Uptowners were surprised; they were out of their element. Now they *know* you're here, they *know* what you're after, and you'll be on their home turf."

He makes more of a show of turning it over in his mind before he blows it off. "Be that as it may, a direct approach will work best. We have more than enough firepower to overwhelm any opposition we encounter."

"Bunker Hill, bro," I say. I'm not the kind of guy who usually says *bro*—which is to say, I'm not a bro—but I figure if I butch it up a bit maybe he'll go for it.

"Excuse me?"

"Bunker Hill? Remember? Redcoats try to take it all lined up in rows and shit? A bunch of Colonials just treat it like a shooting gallery? They don't leave until they run out of ammo?"

I get the feeling either Wakefield never heard of Bunker Hill or that he has no intention of basing his decisions on Revolutionary War battles.

I try another tactic. "You want to get to Grand Central fast? Then let's use the subway tunnels. There's a station at Fifty-Ninth and Fifth. Probably barely guarded. A ten-minute jog and we'll come up beneath those Uptown fools, snatch the football before they know it."

I have no desire whatsoever to relive my time in the subway. Last time I was underground, we were getting chased by the Uptowners through the territory of the Mole People. Things got all Mines of Moria up in that bitch, like, chaos and violence and tragedy and whatnot. Some nice kids died.

We even lost track of Jefferson for a while, and he came back with Kath, all hotsy-totsy and murderous. At the station I just talked about? She shanked a guy to death while she was kissing him. Girl is fierce. Like, actually fierce.

All that aside, it probably would be safer to hit the Bazaar through the tunnels.

Wakefield: "Thank you for your thoughts. Now, if you're done, we'll be getting on."

There's a blanket of snow on the ground, absorbing noise, making the streets hushed and peaceful. The snow keeps coming down like we're inside a cheap souvenir, and burned-out cars and mailboxes and twisted garbage cans get turned into white sculptures. I'm trying to shake the childhood flashbacks—peeking in the Saks Fifth Avenue windows, hot chocolate by the skating rink at Rockefeller Center, horse-drawn carriages. The horses got shot and eaten; the ice rink turned into a swampy pool.

After slinking and juking our way down from the park with nobody saying boo, the soldiers and Gurkhas have loosened up a bit and are taking a cautious stroll down the middle of the street. But around Madison Avenue, the trouble starts, just like I knew it would.

It begins quietly at first. A piece of paper flutters down from above, like a crazy-large snowflake. There's a whole lot of *above* in this part of town, cement and granite and sandstone cliffs studded with pocked and smashed windows, ragged flags and corporate banners trailing and flitting.

I pick up the paper. *Please be advised that garbage collection will shift from Wednesdays to Thursdays beginning on Memorial Day...* I laugh. There are drifts of debris all up and down the street, seething with vermin.

Another leaf of paper floats down. Another. Then the drifts grow into a flurry... a storm. The soldiers look up along their rifle sights, trying to spot who's making this happen.

And suddenly it's not just paper falling from the sky but flat-screen televisions, tables, chairs, metal rectangles that must be computer servers or something. They're easy to dodge because they're coming from way up, but it draws all our attention.

And then the attack begins from down on the ground. The guy next to me—a freckly redhead—goes down, and I hear the thunderous ratcheting of a big machine gun, jostling and screaming, *crack*s of bullets hitting buildings. A piece of debris hits me on the shoulder, and I fall over. I find myself looking into the eyes of the redhead as the light goes out of them. Better him than me.

I crabwalk toward the nearest doorway but find my way blocked by an Uptowner with an old cavalry saber. He charges and whips the sword down at my head, and I only just manage to get my backpack up to block the swing. The sword slashes the bag open, and all my stuff rains around me as I try to recover. Homeboy stabs and hacks at me, chipping his sword against the street as I dodge. It looks like he's gonna carve me until, somehow, he levitates into the air.

At first, I think it's some crazy superpower he's just discovering, but no. He's actually getting lifted up by Donna's former bodyguard. The huge guy straight-up Mr. T's him into a wall, like he's a puppet or something. The Uptowner crumples, leaving a sick red stain on the granite.

I scurry to the doorway, where I'm soon joined by the giant. Down the street, the soldiers have reacted quickly, breaking into two squads and hugging either side of the street.

Ahead, in the direction of Grand Central, I hear more shouting, and the *rat-a-tat* of the guns goes up a notch. One of the little guys with the knives appears, his face spattered with blood. He wipes his knife on his pants.

"Very bad outside!" he says.

I look back the way we came and see a blossom of orange fire and black smoke. It's a flamethrower, for sure. The guy must be positioned around the corner, waiting for us to try to retreat so that he can roast us alive.

"Well," I say, "we're officially fucked."

"Looking that way," says the guy whose name, I now remember, is Titch.

I look through the plate glass of the heavy brass doors, and a lightbulb goes on in my mind. My memory is tweaking back to a shopping expedition long ago, a dull afternoon with Donna that we managed to make fun. We were just wandering around Grand Central, and we realized that there were passages to some of the big buildings nearby so that people could get to their commute straight from their office buildings without going out into the cold winter streets. If we're lucky, this is one of those buildings.

"This way, boys," I say.

The lobby of the old office complex is cavernous and complicated, vaulted and marbled like it's Gotham City or some shit. Tucked in its recesses, there's a little clump of shops to feed the offices above. We pass a dead cafeteria, a news kiosk, a shoe-shine station that sits like an abandoned throne. The surfaces dance in front of our eyes as we flee from the light and the firefight: me, Titch, and the Gurkha named Guja.

And then there, in front of us, is a passageway that leads down into the subway. There's a long, dark, gently inclining tunnel. Two switchbacks leave us off at a tollbooth-and-turnstile vestibule. There's a shutter made of modular steel ribs blocking the corridor. I try to lift it, but the padlocks are rusted shut.

Guja comes over to me and says, "We must go back."

"Back where?" I say. "Back up *there*? You mean back into the shit? What for?"

"Colonel Wakefield. The mission."

"Colonel Wakefield should've listened to me," I respond.

The Gurkha has nothing to say to this, other than "We must go back."

"We don't even know if they're alive."

Guja takes out a little communication device and turns it on. Nothing but static. Which could be because we're underground or could be because everyone up top is dead.

Titch says, "If they're dead, Guja, there's nothing we can do. If they're still alive, then they'll try to complete the mission, and they'll head to the Bazaar, same as before. If they've been taken hostage, they'll end up there anyway. So that's where we go. Okay?"

The Gurkha thinks. Conflict on his face. He doesn't want me to be right. Eventually, he just nods.

I say, "Great, except that we're stuck here. Unless one of you has a bolt cutter."

Titch strides up to the gate and, after peering at the details for a moment or two, places the heel of his boot chest-high against the links, then wraps his gigantic hands around a pair of strengthening rods. He heaves at them, and a series of groans and pops from the metal assembly ends in a section of the gate just ripping away and hanging limply to the ground.

"Shall we?" he says.

RAB

THE RUSSIANS WITHDRAW, TAKING WITH THEM the guy Donna patched up with spit and cello-tape—and how sexy is that, by the way?

I mean Donna's skill, not the taped-together Russki.

We take safer positions and watch as the Russian squad is followed by an equally dangerous-looking crew of what appear to be Chinese commandos—at least, judging by their quick, hushed monosyllables. Which, if you count the Brits and our American cousins together in one mission, raises the total number of world powers currently tootling around New York looking for the biscuit to four. From a strategic point of view, this is not good.

If I were a betting man, I'd reckon that back at HQ they aren't too pleased about the possibility of the US nuclear arsenal falling into the hands of the pugnacious Russians or the godless Chinese commies. This all smacks to me of the possibility of Escalation, of carrier groups and amphibious assault units on the way, of a very large consignment of Shit heading at terminal velocity toward an equally outsize Fan. Judging by the direction the commandos are heading, there will be the proverbial hot time in the old town tonight. The old town being Grand Central, last-known location of the ever-elusive footy. And then? Who knows. Perhaps the global balance of power changes. Or the world ends.

I call Titch up on the walkie to let him know about the Russians and the Chinese but get no response, which either means he's busy or he's dead. It's very hard to imagine anything or anybody killing such a specimen of size and ferocity, so presumably he has better things to do than talk to me.

Though a habitually ungrateful sod, I'm genuinely thankful that Titch has let me take on this side mission, as opposed to, say, crushing my head between his beefy hands à la Gregor Clegane. Perhaps he knows that I'll protect Donna if I can.

Who am I kidding? Donna's the one who'll have to protect me.

We pick up our journey westward, slushing through the snow and shell casings. To our right is the tundra-like expanse of this huge, godforsaken park. To our left, over the trees, mountainous buildings rise, as if all the tallest bits of London from its oil-and-oligarch stage had been crammed together in a small space and had reproduced like rabbits.

We reach the west edge of the park, demarcated by gray stone walls, and head uptown. Wild dogs, a charming feature of the neighborhood, look at us with gustatory curiosity. The snow, mostly unturned by travelers, is silvery and glistening. There's a hush over the whole ruined island.

I observe Jefferson and Donna as they amble along, silent but

THÁL
RAP

xxxxxxx2902

1/20/2021

Item: ï¿½0010087031901 ((book)

companionable. They're together again—but something's up between them. Not just the obvious history. I mean something toxic, a crack I can wedge myself into.

I pry my eyes from the objectionable sight of the two of them together and look around at the buildings. This must have been a fun city at some point—so much sheer density, so much life and commerce in such a small space. Now it's a stinking cyclopean mausoleum. Again I ponder my 100 percent terrible, not-even-so-bad-it's-good decision to come here.

Not that it was *entirely* my choice, of course. A couple of years ago, when I was apprehended by the Reconstruction Committee at the tender age of eighteen, it was made very clear to me that if I did not do the proverbial One Last Job for my esteemed employers, I would be expected to carry water for them for the rest of my days, until I was a Very Old Rab, an even more deeply compromised Rab, a thoroughly de-souled and bitter and worn-out Rabindranath Tagore Tandon. My handlers back home, Welsh and the intelligence gang, are on the surface a pleasant lot. But beneath the velvety smoothness of the public-school-accented talk, one can feel the clenched iron fingers of political zealotry. They're much more committed than any of the flakes and the sport protesters and the guitar-bothering communards I was running with. For all their polish, Welsh and his lot are dangerous animals.

I look around at the heavily armed hormone factories I'm surrounded by. Jefferson and Donna. Kath and the little psychos she has trailing at her heels. And I feel very out of place.

Young Rabindranath is not a zealot. Guileless, unassuming, gentle Rab, who would not hurt whatever it is that malicious flies hurt, let alone a fly, has never felt overly attached to any particular set of principles.

That does not, mind you, mean that I am *un*principled. Rather, I am *over*-principled. I am, to quote your national bard Whitman, "large, I contain multitudes." I can see both sides. For me, life is not just not black-and-white; it is not gray, either. It is a rainbow whose colors and intensities shift as it falls upon different ethical and contextual landscapes.

I'm only a part of this mess at all because the Reconstruction Committee convinced me it might be time to give a little thought to the idea of Political Stability.

Admittedly, this was after they'd apprehended me whilst I was attempting to download encrypted files detailing the Reconstruction Committee's kill list onto a Wi-Fi disk.

"Some part of me is pleased," said Welsh on our first meeting, as he set down his cup and saucer and pulled the government-issue chair over to the metal table, "to see that Trinity has kept up its tradition of treachery. Continuity is a good thing. But only a very small part of me. The rest of me wonders, Rabindranath, what we are to do with you."

What indeed? I was given a choice between languishing in very unpleasant lodgings at His Majesty's pleasure for the foreseeable future, or doing a good turn for the Reconstruction Committee. So I made the only decision I could. Which is to say, I spilled the proverbial beans. I flipped. I flopped. I turned.

Enough with the booing and hissing! How is it my fault? I was not made to be a hero. I was made to live well and to appreciate the finer things, the look on a girl's face at peak moments, the heady buzz of just enough but not too much to drink, soft summer evenings on the River Cam.

So, one fateful day, Welsh, my handler at MI5, found a job suited to a boy of my talents: to seduce a young American girl, fresh from the plague zone, newly arrived on our shores.

At first, the very idea was a shock. We had been informed, or misinformed rather, that there was no cure for the Sickness. This justified the death penalty for any travel to the plague zone (so reminiscent of the prohibition against travel to Talos IV, the planet inhabited by psionic manipulators in the renowned, rejiggered pilot of the original *Star Trek*, first known as "The Cage" and then known as "The Menagerie").

Well, here I am now, on the surface, as it were, of Talos IV. The planet of death and doom. The smoke of a thousand fires climbs the sky. Carrion birds circle the air like it's a roller rink on half-price day.

The good news was, not only have the intrepid scientists of the Reconstruction developed a vaccine for the Sickness but some bunch of post-apocalyptic street urchins in New York had developed their own home-brew version. The bad news was, a stable population in America completely gazumps the British authorities, who had planned to resume their colonial tendencies and begin anew in the Old New World after mourning the dead for an efficiently appropriate period of time.

So—my mission was to insinuate myself into the trust of the escaped tomboy. She was to be placed at Trinity College Cambridge under an alias.

Unbeknownst to said dystopian nymphet, I was to befriend and if possible *befriend* her, and report back any findings to my puppet masters.

Donna proved to be quite a vexing assignment, what with her haunted, postlapsarian grief, her stubborn loyalty to absent tribe and paramour. What was I to do? She was too much of a coil even for me to unravel.

I complained to my superiors, and they came up with an idea guaranteed to set her fully adrift and leave me as the only harbor in her grief: They killed off her friends. Or at least they made Donna *believe* that her tribe had been killed. It was most likely that they *had* died anyway, given the hurly-burly that I understood the United States to be. At any rate, that was the cut that finally brought her down; it was also, ironically, to be my comeuppance. I didn't expect that, in witnessing her suffering, her deep and unalloyed pain, I would fall for her.

That is my embarrassing revelation: that, after all this, I have to admit that I am, unfortunately, in love with Donna. Presumably hopelessly, as she has taken the news that I was playacting rather hard.

Hard? Diamonds are hard. This is something else.

Spare a kindly thought for poor Rab, dusting flecks of broken window off his natty camo anorak, wondering how he's going to manage to get out of this alive. How was I to know that I would fall in love? Nothing in life had prepared me for such an accident.

Which is why I find myself off-piste, as it were, creeping through muck and snow behind a granite wall, on an utterly pointless mission to rescue some damsels in distress. Not even damsels I'm interested in. Utterly arbitrary damsels, useless damsels, may-as-well-be-blokes damsels. But what can I do? I'm in love.

And she's in love with someone else.

The posse stops for a breather, and Donna and Jefferson stop orbiting each other for a nanosecond. As soon as Donna is out of earshot, I stroll over to him.

"My name is Rab," I say, holding out my paw.

Jefferson looks at it and smiles, as if I've just swept off my plumed hat with a spiral flourish as I bowed low to the ground. He grasps it in his filthy, calloused mitt.

"I know," he says. "Donna's friend."

He doesn't say "friend" in any particularly provocative way. But it definitely puts me on the qui vive.

"Nice place you've got here," I say, gesturing at the stinking wreckage of a city.

"Do you think so?" he says.

"No. Sorry. I was being ironic."

"I figured. It used to be something." We walk on a bit, the wall to our left, the ground dipping and rising. Donna is looking over suspiciously but wants no part of this conversation, it seems. "I went to England once. When my brother and I were little."

"Changing of the Guard? Madame Tussaud's?"

He shakes his head. "The John Soane museum. Brick Lane. Clerkenwell." He even says it right, "CLARK-en-well." He shrugs. "My parents were weird. I liked the salt beef bagels."

I really want to dislike this guy, I do.

"Anyway," he says, "thank you for helping Donna. She's…she's unique. Isn't she?"

I want to say something clever and deflating. But all I can say is "Yes."

He fishes around in a bag. Hands me a pistol.

"This is a dangerous place. Not smart to go unarmed," he says. He waves off my protests. "Oh, I have plenty. Give it back to me when we're done."

"When are we done?" I say.

"Don't know," he says.

I look at the gun. Wakefield and the others, *my side*, did not trust me to carry one. And they want me to kill the boy who's offering me one of his own.

Those are my orders: At all costs, sparing no harm to my companions or myself, ensure that any nuclear capability represented by the football is mitigated or, failing that, any and all copies of the launch codes are destroyed— including those in the memory of anyone I encounter. That last article, as I have been realizing, enjoins me to kill anyone who has had even the briefest contact with the football, since they might have been *capable* of memorizing the codes. Which means that Donna's young swain Jefferson is on the chopping block. Wakefield would have done it if he had time and occasion to do it out of Donna's sight, I expect; or maybe they don't want blood on official hands. They're like that.

Can *I* do it? That sort of business is somewhat outside my experience, but they did teach me, back at Central Office, how to end things quickly and painlessly, at least according to them, using little more than the nifty little dagger they've given me. It looks like a letter opener, only triangular in cross section. I believe it is meant to produce a puncture wound that refuses to stop bleeding. Physically, I can do it. But morally?

I know I should hate him, but Jefferson has his points. If I'm the summer blockbuster, the tentpole of guys, he's good counterprogramming, the indie darling. If he and I had lived down the staircase from each other, he'd have made a great wingman, and might even draw off a few of the starry-eyed girls whose intuitions about my callowness were borne out by catching me in a compromising position or two.

And I daresay Jefferson has done a lot of things *right*, if right and wrong are the sort of thing you care about. But at any rate, there were no moral riders attached to my Faustian, Bondian contract to kill.

And now the boy who's supposed to be my target is giving me the tool to do the deed. This is not emotionally convenient. Time and tide may require me to murder him, which does not sit well. For one thing, I find myself liking him. For another, I find it galling that my actions could be mistaken for those of a jilted rival.

Jefferson sidles up to Donna again, and I find someplace else to look. I scan the solemn avenues of wrecked buildings, the white wilderness of the park, and try to imagine my way, through it all, back into Donna's mind, and maybe from there into her heart. Here I am in, to quote the good old King James Version, "the abomination of desolation."

But the mountains and hills, or rather, the high-rises and skyscrapers, have not been laid low. They are still standing, only a little marred by the actions of fire and weather and vandalous teens. This is what the Reconstruction Committee wants back—the houses and flats and offices. They want all of it, the whole nation, to extract the oil and iron and anything else they can suck from it. It seems, to me, blasphemous—not that blasphemy has ever been something to frighten me. But how many ghosts must there be here? The whole city is a haunted house.

We head up the less-than-imaginatively-named Central Park West, ears pricked. Since I have no idea what to look for, I take the time to ponder Kath, the preposterously gorgeous blond with two blond little flunkies at her heels. Anytime up to the near present, young Rab would have bent all his energy and skill to the task of securing some private time with such a dish. But now, to my amazement, I find that I have no interest. The conceptual framework is there—I understand how attractive she is, the curves and planes and hollows speak to me in a language I well remember—but the visceral charge is gone.

I crave only Donna. Her black eyes, her high-bridged nose, everything down to her slender little feet. But more, what she contains: Her laughter. Her thoughts. Her mind. Her spirit. It is a terrible thing, to find my talents suitable to any purpose but the essential one. I feel like a skeleton key that works in every door but the one I'm trying to get through.

Enough, my soul. Put aside such thoughts. Concentrate, rather, on not getting killed.

In the middle distance stretches a massive neoclassical pile, which can only be the aforesaid museum. I gather that it contains, like its British cousin, various skeletal dinosaurs and stuffed wildebeests and simulated Neanderthal domestic scenes.

And if our information is correct, a modern-day slave market. Charming.

We slip over the wall of the park for cover while we have a bit of a chin-wag. "Kath," says Jefferson, "time to tell us everything you know."

"I don't really know many details. I never went," she says. "I mean, I had my own problems, right? I didn't *want* to know."

Donna says, "You mean *you* were doing okay, so you didn't give a shit what happened to anybody else."

Kath looks as though she's about to contradict her, but then she just says, "Yeah, pretty much."

She tells us what she *does* know. The name of the tribe controlling the west side of Manhattan, and thus the museum, is the OGs. Despite the seeming reference to rap and blaxploitation films, said OGs are actually white kids. Control of the slave market was a concession that the Uptowners made to maintain peace so that they could concentrate on their closest enemies, the Harlemites, who are, in fact, black, or as they would say here, African American. The Uptowners retained control of the market in petrol and food. Shelter, it would seem, is not an issue, as thousands of houses and flats remain uninhabited. But how will they survive the winter?

I have a question. "So—sorry if I'm being naive, but what, exactly, are these slaves used for? I mean, nobody's growing cotton, right?"

There's a pause. Probably I have put things the wrong way. I never knew the ins and outs of America's tortured and tortuous relationship with slavery, only that most Americans wanted to avoid talking about it. Of course, Britain was every bit as involved, happily dashing about the globe shipping human beings here and there for profit, until the profit margins fell. But—

"It's not about *work*," says Kath.

"You mean…"

"I mean sex. I mean rape."

Kath laughs at what must be the shocked expression on my face.

"Oh, come *on*," she says. "Are you surprised?"

"Surprised?" I think it over. "No. I suppose I'm not. But I'm disgusted."

Kath makes a noise best rendered as *pfffft!* that presumably indicates her skepticism.

"Like you wouldn't have done the same thing, all you fancy public school pricks."

Kath, I can see, has also traveled. This makes sense. She has a certain Courchevel après-ski look to her, a private-jet-set vibe.

"Young lady," I say, "I may not be the most *evolved* of males, but *consent* is the salt to my meat. Without that, we're just animals."

I am in, if not a white-hot rage, at least an off-white rage, or, shall we say, a handsomely tawny-colored rage. I think, perhaps, if I am let loose on the museum with a gun, I will have a chance to practice up for any less justified murders to follow.

We creep along the wall until we can see, on the steps of the museum, a little convocation of boys with guns. I fetch out my government-issue binoculars for a better look and spy, beneath a decaying gargantuan scorpion model that was mounted above the portico in better days, presumably to attract and repel schoolchildren, the guards, curiously done up in tattered robes. Stranger still, they appear to be sporting long beards beneath faces clearly still youthful and collagen-rich. As though they were going to a fancy dress ball having chosen a rather dubious Islamic State theme, for which they will later be made to apologize.

"We don't have the firepower to force our way in and out," reiterates Jefferson.

"Good. I don't like to go anyplace I'm not invited, especially if they'll shoot me."

So the guns are definitely real, then, even if the beards aren't. Not terribly surprising given that there was one firearm for every man, woman, and child in the country before the Sickness hit. I'm not 100 percent sure what led to this peculiar state of affairs. I suppose after all it was the fault of my countrymen, the British, for getting ourselves beaten by a bunch of bloody-minded, overarmed farmers. If your country gets its debut because everybody and their uncle Zebediah has a blunderbuss, you get to rating guns pretty highly.

Same thing goes for human bondage. There are millions of people enslaved in modern, progressive, technologically switched-on India to this day, working off debts or crimes for the grievous and unpardonable sin of being born into the wrong caste. The British, who in theory abolished slavery in the middle of the nineteenth century, basically just renamed it. I ought to know, for my people were bureaucrats and organizers of imperial infrastructure great and small, veritable Uncle Tom–jis, which is how I ended up, like many of my ancestors, at Eton and Cambridge.

Well, Rab, you have worked yourself into a fine moral lather, haven't you? Let that stiffen your spine in the hours to come.

"Come again?" say I. I have not been taking everything in.

Donna looks annoyed. "I *said*, so we need to think of another way in, then."

"Do we really?" It seems a question worth asking.

"I can't expect you to understand," says Donna. "It's not your tribe." Her look, not spiteful, only indifferent, tears at my gut.

"Well," I say, "how about a little subterfuge? Give the good old Chewbacca maneuver a go? We escort in a fake prisoner?"

"Can't say it's the worst idea," says Jefferson.

"Yeah, but there's no way we can guarantee that somebody won't recognize you. You're public enemy number one." Donna smiles at Jefferson. Damnation.

"I'll go," I find myself saying, and immediately regret it. Really, this is too much. There is no point to impressing Donna with my heroism if I die in the process. I want to be alive to enjoy the fruits of my labor. I am hoping that someone will say something along the lines of *No, this isn't your fight!*

But there are no takers. Instead, Kath says, "I'll be Chewbacca."

"No, Mommy!" whine her two little blond shadows. "Stay with us!"

Donna says, "It's my tribe. I should go."

"You?" Kath snorts. "No offense, but who do you think people would want to buy more, you or me?"

Kath's point is one of the more perverse I've ever seen expressed, but she's not wrong, I suppose. With her flaxen hair and rosy cheeks, she's a regular harem-member *manquée*. That notwithstanding, she's a loose cannon, and besides, I have other ideas.

"Donna goes," I say.

The others look at me. *Yes,* I stare back at them, *I can make arbitrary decisions, too.*

"It's *her* tribe. And it's *my* neck. So Donna goes with me."

Maybe things will get hairy and I'll get the chance to jump in front of a crossbow bolt to save her, a showy but easily reparable wound—taped up by the fair hands of Donna herself, preferably—that will shift the needle of public opinion in my direction.

Donna is not happy about this arrangement, though. It implies a sort of relationship between her and me, a *partner*ship.

But she does not make that objection outwardly, which tells me that she and Jefferson have not had The Talk, the one in which she breaks it to Jefferson that she and I have slept together. I hope it's just that she's saving the news for a good enough argument. More likely, she just can't stand the idea of telling him and spoiling their glorious sodding reunion.

Well, that doesn't stop me from dropping hints, does it?

"And if you ask *me*," I say, my expression implying that I'm speaking from experience, "Donna is *plenty* desirable."

Donna looks at me with utter contempt. Never mind. To make an omelette, one must annoy some eggs.

Jefferson has nothing to say to this. I seem to have carried the point with sheer bravado.

So. Over the wall, down the cobbled parkside pavement, across the street to the grand stairs and portico. The bearded boys look down at us with the studied, trigger-fondling disdain of movie gunsels. Donna, loosely zip-tied and led by the elbow, has her eyes down. The guards address themselves to me.

"Sale isn't till Sunday," says one of them. And I notice that his ZZ Topp look is the result of his having strung hair extensions into his best-but-still-lacking, undergrowth-like efforts at an actual beard.

I resist the urge to laugh. I tell myself, Rab, who are you to question the tonsorial choices of this young gentleman, who is a person like you, and at the same time, a special snowflake unlike any other? Also, I make it my business not to laugh at people carrying Kalashnikovs.

His colleagues are equally bebearded, in extremist rather than hipster fashion. Something, I tell myself, is up. I quickly take in the jingling metal symbols dangling like charms from their necks. Cross, Star of David, crescent. Like a version of those Coexist bumper stickers that found their way to London before the Sickness. Curious.

At any rate, I realize that Donna is not going to supply a response to the young thug's statement, as she is meant to be a cowed and depressed victim. So I say, "Yeah, I know. I came early to check out the competition. Wanna see what kind of price I can get."

"You sound funny," says another little slavemonger, which is rather rich, given that he sounds like the arse end of a clarinet played through the nostril. But now is not the time to be undiplomatic.

"I'm from Jersey," I say, a response that, I have been told, will cover any sort of irregularity.

And indeed, it works. The creeps would rather pretend to be sophisticated than venture to quiz me on, say, the popular pastimes and landmarks of New Jerseyans, which, judging only from my exposure to *The Sopranos*, largely involve dumping bodies and eating mozzarella.

"How're those Jersey girls?" asks one kid.

"See for yourself," I say. I take Donna's chin in my hand and tilt her face upward. I can't tell if the micro-glance of hatred she gives me is genuine or playacting. If it's the latter, she's doing it well. But she must understand that I'm just trying to put on a convincing front. Perhaps it's my facility with lying that puts her in mind of past peccadilloes.

The bearded boys take a look at her, up and down, male gazes unfettered by any social constraint.

"How much?" says one. "We'll take her off your hands."

"Mmmm, I think I'll trust the full price-setting power of the market."

"How about we rent her for an hour?"

Even I, smooth and supple liar that I am, feel my bile rise and find myself at a pause.

"Thanks," I say. "But I'd like to keep the merchandise in prime condition, and you fellows look a bit rough."

They laugh, the closest one holds up his hand for a fist bump, and, to my eternal shame, I comply. I have a brief mental image of his hand, in a graphically rendered version of the imaginary follow-through, exploding in a fine red mist.

"Go on in, chief," he says.

Donna and I head up the stairs. She turns to me and says, sotto voce, "I'm going to fucking kill all of them."

I'm a bit taken aback; this is not the Donna who sat next to me on Dr. Maule's couch and elucidated the distinction between back-formation and folk etymology.

"Do you mean kill, in the sense that people used to mean it, as in you really hate them, or do you mean *kill* kill?"

She looks at me and leaves no doubt.

I open the door for her—even if I weren't a gentleman, there's the fact that her hands are zip-tied behind her back. We find ourselves in a big lobby, wall-to-wall marble, real nineteenth-century American inferiority complex–grade expense and bombast. Another creep with his feet up behind what used to be the ticket booth. Discounts for students and senior citizens, etc.

Beardy looks at us glassy-eyed, presumably due to whatever superpowered Stash he's smoking, which also stinks up the place. Barely rousing himself from his seat long enough to ogle Donna, he waves us through.

We walk into an anteroom, past huddled fighters still asleep from the previous night's revels. They all wear those same beards, the detached extension pieces and outright panto-level fakes sometimes laid beside them like shed clothing.

Then, revealed through a tall arch, we enter a fairly magnificent atrium, churchy in its way, and there before us is a brontosaurus (or apatosaurus for all you dino snobs) and, as though caught in midstride, dear old T. rex, everyone's favorite vicious carnivore.

How I used to love him. Fierce and brutal and utterly unconcerned with anything but his own appetites, just like me as a little boy. Meat-eaters were always my favorite, since I was required to be vegetarian. I delighted in nature programs on the old Zenith back at the family house (more like a compound really) in Kolkata. Mama thought I had an empathetic regard for animals that bespoke a deep and burgeoning spirituality. I did not tell her the real reason I loved the programs. It was a reimagining of the social contract. Snacking on the neighbors, getting rid of your sister, commanding the attention of all the ladies...All these possibilities appealed to a five-year-old solipsist.

There's commotion from afar, filtered and echoed through brick-floored chambers. Then a voice yells what sounds like "Feeding time!"

Surely that can't be it?

"Did you just hear that?" I ask Donna.

Donna deigns to speak to me. "Yes."

"What did you hear?"

"Feeding time." Then, "Let's go see."

"Feeling a bit peckish myself," I say.

DONNA

EASING OUR WAY TOWARD THE sounds, we come to a big vaulted room, like a giant lung, with a high glass-paneled ceiling emitting sour blue light. There are panes missing in the glass, making for a surreal scene: There's a life-size blue whale suspended from the rafters, and snow falls down around it. The whale is maybe a hundred feet long, its massive frame taking up the length of the chamber while its underslung jaw is tilted down and facing us.

Along the walls, big picture windows are lined with rows of what look like giant aquarium tanks. At one time, they must have been illuminated, but now they are dark and foreboding.

Rab and I approach the nearest one, his hand on my wrist. We're trying to keep up the pretense that he's going to sell me. Where his flesh touches mine, I feel a buzz, though I can't tell if it's one of annoyance or attraction. My emotional compass has gone all haywire, pinging around love and hate like a needle at the North Pole.

I see a pod of dolphins frozen in midswim through waves of Plexiglas water. Tuna flee, and seagulls hang in the air above, hoping for scraps. A cocktail-colored sunset is painted behind them. It must have been a pretty striking diorama at some point, but now the solid surface of the ocean is scattered with debris, and one of the birds hangs awkwardly from its invisible moorings.

I'm looking at the faux setting sun when I see movement in the back of the display.

There's something huddled against the far corner, hiding from the light. As I peer further, my eyes adjust, and I see—

"Oh God," says Rab.

It's a cluster of girls, half naked, huddled together for warmth like a clutch of tree frogs. Their eyes, the pinballing eyes of prey, peer out from grimy faces. I try to recognize somebody from the tribe, but it's too dark, the faces too frightened and gaunt to make out in the dark.

A slop of garbage falls from a jagged square hole in the ceiling above the display. It plops onto the surface of the ocean, tumbling off the static dolphins.

And the girls scramble forward to eat.

Boy's voice: "I love feeding time." I turn to see a boy in

taped-together glasses. He's talking to Rab, occasionally flashing a look at my chest. "It's the only thing that really makes them come out and give you a good look at them." He's bearded up like the rest but surprisingly jolly.

Rab: "Doesn't look too healthy for them."

Boy: "Well, honestly, who's eating well these days?" He sidles up to the case and peers in at the girls. He taps at the window.

Then he looks sidelong at me, I guess taking my look of disgust for concern.

Boy: "Oh, don't worry. Sale's on Sunday. You won't have to spend long in there. Not a nice one like you."

I look to Rab.

Me: "Him too."

Rab nods. The boy looks confused.

Boy: "What does she mean?"

Rab: "Can you tell me something?" He points at the crescent, cross, and star hanging over the boy's belly. "That stuff. The symbols. What do they mean? You'll have to forgive my ignorance. I've come all the way from New Jersey."

Boy (chuckles): "Oh, that. That's the Fundaments."

Rab: "How so?"

Boy: "That's what we believe in here. The Fundaments. See, we've spent too much time hating on each other for our beliefs. We realized we need to recognize the deep similarities in all the major world religions."

Rab: "Peace, love thy neighbor, charity, all that?"

Boy: "No, not that. I mean the primacy of the masculine gender."

Rab: "Oh."

There's a hole in my gut that I want to fill up with violence.

Boy: "What did peace and love and charity do for us?"

Rab: "I thought they gave life meaning."

Boy: "Nah. They made us weak. That's how we got here."

Rab: "I thought we got here because somebody released a killer virus."

Boy: "Yes, but *why*? Because we didn't eliminate our enemies. If we had, there would have been nobody to release the virus on or to release the virus on us. With the Fundaments, we've united all peoples."

Rab: "Except the people you haven't united."

The kid shrugs.

Boy: "Give us time." He makes a looking-at-his-watch gesture, although he doesn't have a watch. "Well, gotta go. But you'll see me again. I'll definitely be in the market for *this* one."

He means me.

I definitely hope we meet again.

Rab: "Thanks."

As he saunters off, I follow the boy with my eyes and see him join another cluster of bearded thugs.

Rab: "Let's get out of here."

Me: "Not yet. I haven't seen our people."

Rab: "Does it matter? Look how many of them there are." He nods up toward the gallery above, where I can see more and more of the slavers, all of them sporting guns. "These people are *psychos. And* armed. And more than we can handle."

I want to hate him for being a coward, but the truth is that he's right. If we're going to crack this place, we need some major firepower. But I'm not in the mood to agree with him.

Me: "What else is new?" I walk along the rows of cases. In one, a sperm whale fights a giant squid. In another, a walrus family perches on a drift of ice.

Then I stop. I walk slowly up to the filthy pane of glass.

One of the naked figures inside looks up and stops eating. She crawls over to the glass.

The girl's voice through the glass is gravelly, scarred. It's Carolyn. From my tribe. Her beautiful hair is matted, her cheeks sunken. Her sweet voice is broken.

Carolyn: "Donna! Donna!"

I shake my head, telling her to be quiet. But she doesn't stop. She cries and slams her palms against the glass.

Carolyn: "They got you, too. Oh, they got you, too. Oh, Donna."

I look around… The sound is echoing through the hall. Some of the slavers look up.

I'm crying now, trying to hold my body erect and proud, to show the girls inside that I'm not beaten. I try to whisper to her through the glass.

Me: "No. I have a plan. We're coming back. We're coming back."

Finally, Carolyn stops hitting the glass and turns to scrabble for food with the others. I don't know if she understood me.

The slavers are drifting over toward us, thumbing their safeties.

Rab grabs ahold of my arm and drags me out of the gallery.

Once they see him manhandling me, their suspicions are put to rest. And my tears, as it turns out, complete the disguise. The slavers smile indulgently at me, as if these things, these curious phenomena, the emotions of others, were the inconveniences of the trade.

JEFFERSON

KATH AND I WAIT BEHIND the park wall. The Thrill Kill Twins are throwing snowballs by the trees. I feel a strange urge to join them.

I remember being that age, just a few years ago, when you could go either way, kid or adult, even oscillate between the two many times in the course of a day. I think about the harmless violence of a snowball fight and wonder what the appeal can be when people are lobbing actual rocks at one another. Absently, my hands make a snowball, cupping the powder, forming the sphere. I dig down too deep, and the snowball gets dirty.

"Not too late to leave," says Kath. She's been observing me.

"Leave for where?"

"The island. You remember, on the *Annie*? Those little outposts on the Sound . . . those messed-up vegetables they were growing?"

"They looked messed-up because they were grown by hand, not by some automated industry."

"Well, they tasted good," she says. "And that chicken…and the good wine…"

"Yeah," I say. I remember. A moment of almost freedom.

"We could go," says Kath. "Just you and me. Go and work on one of those farms. We can live."

Live. Not just survive.

I turn to her. "I couldn't leave the others."

"You mean you couldn't leave *her*." She says that without any rancor.

I don't say anything to that.

"But you could," she says. "Don't you see it?"

She waits for me to finish the thought. What don't I see?

She helps. "Rab. Her and Rab."

And I know that it's true. I know it.

Can I hold that against Donna? No. But that doesn't keep me from feeling a deep scoring in my chest, a pain like being hungrier than I've ever been. Like nothing will ever be okay again.

"If you and I leave, she'll be all right. She'll have Rab. What if you stay and she goes with Rab? Do you want to be left holding the bag? Better to go now."

"The girls from my tribe—"

"There's no way, Jefferson. The slavers are too strong. What are we? Six people, low on ammo, half starving. Can't happen."

She looks away. Then looks back.

"And I love you," she says. "There's that."

I look at Kath now, her blue eyes shining out of the grime. I feel like I'm holding her heart in my hand; I can feel all the scars and spikes.

"You might be right," I say. "Maybe she's gone. Maybe it should be you and me."

She frowns. "There's a 'but' coming."

"But. I have to do one small thing that's right and honest, even if it kills me," I say. "I have to try to get our people free. I can't see any further than that right now."

She looks down. Nods. "I shouldn't stay, then. This isn't my tribe. And you don't love me. So I don't love you back. I should go."

But she doesn't.

I reach out and take her hand.

There's the sound of footsteps, muffled by snow, on the other side of the wall. We raise our guns and peer over. There's Donna and Rab. Rab is leaning over Donna, cutting the zip ties that bind her hands. His hair hangs down and touches hers.

Donna climbs over the wall, notices Kath and me sitting close together and the others paused midthrow. Her face is clouded with—what? Grief? Confusion?

"So?" says Kath.

"Too many of them," says Donna. "There's no way we can get them out of there unless we have more firepower."

"I could have told you that," says Kath. She looks at me, rein-forcing her point.

"They have them behind glass," says Donna. "Like animals. Naked. Starving."

"They'll clean them up for the auction," puts in Kath.

"Whose side are you on, exactly?" asks Donna.

"I told you a long time ago. Mine."

"So what happens next?" says Rab.

Nobody has anything to say.

"We follow whoever gets our people after they buy them," I say.

"And then what? We can't do the same for all of them," says Donna. "It's all or nothing."

All or nothing.

Finally, I say, "I know what we need to do." Everyone looks to me.

But it might be more dangerous than the museum.

The twins race ahead of us up Central Park West, laughing and hollering.

"Mommy! Look! Mommy! Look! I can run right over a car!" The girl does just that, jumping onto the back of a BMW, clomping right over it, springing to the car parked in front without touching the ground.

"Cut that out!" shouts Kath. "If you break an ankle, I'm going to have to put you down." She seems serious about it.

"Aw, you're zero fun!" shouts Abel, the boy.

"I'm not *here* to be *fun*," says Kath, curiously mom-ish annoyance on her face. She's been in a foul mood since we decided to head up to Harlem.

"Are you okay?" I ask.

"I'm fine," she says.

I should know better. I always find myself asking a girl if she's okay when she clearly isn't, and then I fail to understand *I'm fine* for what it means, which is *Leave me alone*.

I silently keep pace with her for a little while. Then I go ahead and say, "We never talked about what it was actually *like* in Uptown, did we?"

"Nope," she says. Strike two.

"So—were there friends of yours that they made, you know, slaves?"

"If by 'slave,' you mean someone over whom you have the power of life and death, who is required to do your bidding, then yes."

"What else would I mean?"

"I used to have this discussion with Theo," Kath says. "He kind of objected to the use of the term, in an American context, because it had its *own specific resonance*. I think that was how he put it. He said that to accuse the Uptowners of slavery was to devalue the term, since to him it referred to a carefully maintained economic and governmental system by which the United States as we knew it was brought into being. Whereas what my brother and the rest were doing in the Bazaar was nothing more than a bunch of armed psychotics indulging themselves."

"I'm not sure I see the difference."

"Well, he didn't like that I thought I was in the same boat as his ancestors just because I got treated like shit, too. I told him he just didn't want to care because it was a bunch of *white* chicks getting exploited."

"Sounds like you guys didn't get along too well. Are you worried about seeing him?"

Kath ponders the imminent possibility for a moment.

"Actually," she says, "we got on just fine. Just because we didn't see eye to eye didn't mean he stopped treating me like a person. I hope he hasn't kicked the bucket."

"Wow," I say. "Sentimental of you." We walk a little farther, the middle-class conveniences of the Upper West Side starting to give way to bodegas and dorms of the old Columbia University precincts.

I observe her a moment—her powder-blue eyes following the pranks of her little wards. Something has changed about her. I think back to long ago, under the ground, when we met—at gunpoint, then grappling. Somehow it ended in kissing. An impromptu bout of making out that was all the more surprising since I was convinced at the time that I was in love with Donna.

Which I still am.

I am.

DONNA

I OBSERVE JEFFERSON AND KATH in the white gloom of the winter day, their shadows occasionally merging as they walk, touching but not touching. The moisture of their breath mingles. I wonder if they're talking about old times.

While I was away.

Can I blame them? For whatever happened? Sometimes I feel like my perspective has zoomed out, like God put his thumb and forefinger on the screen and widened the view.

Because, after all, if you had asked me a year ago if there could ever be anyone for me other than Jefferson, I would have said hell no, and thought that you were a dick for even asking.

And then along came Rab. And did Rab being in my life mean that I was wrong about Jefferson? No. I might have thought that for a moment or two, in my bedroom in Cambridge, in Rab's arms. And I felt so guilty that I cried.

But I don't blame myself now. I was so alone. I used what I had to. I used *who* I had to.

I look over at Rab, walking with his long strides, craning his head this way and that, still not used to the sheer ruin of it all. Seeing him like this, it's hard to keep my anger intact.

In a way, we all use each other. Because we can never really know each other. No matter what you do, everything that happens, everything you think and feel about someone, is filtered through your own perceptions—your *youness*. Maybe you can feel what it's *like* to be other people, but you never *are* them.

So when somebody says, *I love you*, you can never really know what they mean by it, even if you think you know what you mean when you say it to them. You can't even know if *they* think they mean it. All that you can know for sure is that they said those words. So what, eventually, do you have to go on? Only what's in your head.

Once, in school, these Indonesian puppeteers came in to do an assembly. Their puppets were flat, controlled by sticks from below, not strings from above. And the puppets were these amazing works of art, like gorgeously painted leather cutouts. But when you watched, you didn't look at the puppets, you looked at the *shadows* that the puppets cast on a screen because they did the performance in the dark, by the light of an oil lamp.

The way I figure it, most of the time, that's all we see—the image of other people's thoughts and actions, like the shadows on the screen. And because of the way the world works, we don't see the real color of things, and the shapes can be distorted. Maybe every once in a while we see the truth of things, the beauty of the puppets. But most of the time, we just see the screen. And the screen *isn't* the world. It's only how we see the world.

Is it too much to want to stop seeing the shadows, and see the puppets? To see the beautiful painted figures rather than the negative space?

Rab slows down to walk next to me, stumbling for a moment on the bloated corpse of a dog.

Rab: "Well, this is another fine mess."

I'm not in the mood for the shadows he's throwing.

Me: "What do you want?"

Rab walks along, turning over the question with a bemused smile on his face.

Rab: "A whole lot of things. Getting out of this alive, for one. But mostly, I'd like you to talk to me."

He looks at me with a frankness that almost doesn't seem fabricated.

Me: "I just did. Satisfied?"

Rab: "No. Of course, by saying 'talk to me,' what I really meant was, 'Engage with me as though I were a person worth talking to, someone whose care and attention you value.'"

Me: "*Care and attention?* Is that what they called it back at headquarters? When they were giving you your orders?"

Rab: "No. All they said is that I should befriend you."

I manage a scornful "Hah!" while inside, I am feeling even worse about our relationship, if you can call it that, than ever. Somehow I find it more acceptable that Rab would have been assigned to *seduce* me than to become my friend. *That* just makes me feel like a loser. Be*friend*. Jeez.

Me: "Wow. So I guess that by having *sex* with me, you were just going the extra mile for your bosses, huh? You're a regular employee of the month."

Rab: "Good one. No. That was for me. I wanted to. I couldn't help myself."

We've been through this before. Rab claiming that he fell for me as a side effect of insinuating himself into my company. It's an old chestnut, as they'd say back in England. The whole I-started-out-pretending-but-before-I-knew-it-I-wasn't-pretending routine.

Rab: "Why do you think I'm here, Donna?"

Me: "I think you're here because Welsh told you to go. I don't know, maybe you're supposed to trick some other poor ditz into being your *friend*."

I hope he catches hold of the extra mustard I put onto that word.

Rab: "I'm here because I care about you. I wanted to . . . I don't know, to protect you."

This is a laugh. The last time Rab tried to "protect" me, he nearly got the shit beaten out of him. I had to cripple a couple of townies to get his fat out of the fire. Still. Just because he *can't* protect me, it doesn't follow that he doesn't *want* to. Boys think that way sometimes.

Rab: "Donna, if you really don't feel anything . . . if everything you felt for me is gone, then I'll leave you alone."

Me: "It's gone."

Rab falls silent for a moment. Then: "I don't believe you."

I make a show of being annoyed but, really, *are* they all gone? Them feels? Because if Rab ended up feeling more than he had expected, so did I. The thing is, part of me *knew* that Rab couldn't be for real. But there was another part that didn't care because it wanted him. And I went into it thinking that I would get some comfort, some attention, some warmth, some pleasure. So I told myself I could wall off my heart. Let in the physical, keep out the emotional.

But it didn't work that way. And when I found out he'd been sent to spy on me, it ripped up all sorts of things, like most of the wires that connected us . . . but all of them? No. Pulses of feeling are coming through the lines, little signals and codes and transmissions.

I look ahead to where I can vaguely see the outlines of Jefferson and Kath as they walk and talk. Are they hashing things over the way Rab and I are? Have we gone beyond love triangle to love parallelogram? It *is* a fine mess.

Rab: "He isn't what I thought he'd be."

I look to him for explanation even though I know who he's talking about.

Rab: "I thought he'd be . . . I don't know, a paragon of virtue. The way you talked about him. Seven feet tall, radiating light."

Now this pisses me off. It's one thing trying to get back into my, you know, *good graces*. It's another thing entirely to take a shot at Jeff.

Me: "He's a better man than you'll ever be."

Rab smiles, pivots, does a bit of his conversational judo.

Rab: "Oh, that's probably true. Look, you think I'm being unkind because I'm jealous. But I like him *better* this way. Nobody deserves to be idolized. It's a terrible fate."

I make a face, like I'm onto his tricks, like I disagree, but of course he has to be right; it *is* terrible to feel that you have to face up to expectations that you can't possibly meet. I suppose that's why it took me so long to come around to Jefferson in the first place. I mean, not to loving him, but to *his* loving *me*. Like by thinking so highly of me, loving me so much, *he* was somehow lesser. Like maybe he didn't see me because he saw me differently from the way I saw myself. Of course, I was assuming that I saw myself accurately, instead of in the funhouse mirror of my own fuckedupness.

And now that I consider it, *was* Jefferson even who I thought? How could he have left our people to rot—or *worse* than that—while he tried to jury-rig some kind of half-assed Utopia?

But actually, that's *exactly* Jefferson. He *would* hope for the best, and he *would* try to chart the most optimistic course through this sea of blood.

And that's exactly why he really needed me around—to slap some sense into him. An idealist can be every bit as dangerous to, like, the common good as a predator.

I realize that Rab is looking at me, maybe assessing the effect of his words, like a chef inhaling the aroma of an ingredient he's just added to the dish. And he *has* done something, I admit. He shifted Jefferson somehow in my perceptions.

I used to think feelings were just feelings and nothing could change them, least of all words. But words, even though they're light as air, thicken into ideas, add up into actions, and actions *do* move things.

Me: "Stop."

Rab takes it as a rebuff, but that's not what I mean. What I actually mean is, like, stop *walking*.

There's a barely visible wire extended across the street, from the corner of the park to the junked car on the other side.

I hold up my hands, and everybody stops in a line, before hitting the trip wire.

I hear the staticky cough of a walkie-talkie. I look up and around, and see telltale little gleams of plastic and metal. I turn to the others.

Me: "I think now would be a good time to put our guns on the ground and get on our knees."

Kath: "The hell are you talking about?" She doesn't see what I'm noticing.

Then they appear, five of them from behind the park wall, five popping up from their perches in the buildings to the north, another five from straight ahead out of a box truck they're using as a checkpoint. Rifle barrels all focused on us.

I put my gun down and kneel, and the others do accordingly. I shout to the approaching Harlemites.

Me: "We want to speak to Solon."

After a pause, a familiar voice, deep and rumbly, comes back:

Theo: "So do I."

He emerges from behind a parked car and strolls up to the wire.

Me: "Theo."

Theo: "Donna. Long time."

I want to give him a hug, but two things prevent me. One, the trip wire. Two, Theo's manner, which is, like, Switzerland at best. Leaning toward Venezuela. The guns are still up and pointed at us.

Theo: "Solon's gone. Nobody knows where." He looks at Jefferson. "I see you're still hanging out with some ratched-ass company."

Kath: "Is that any way to welcome me back?"

Theo sees Kath for the first time. He cracks a smile.

Theo: "What's up, girl? Glad you're alive. And the twins."

Anna and Abel: "Hi, Theo!"

Theo waves at the twins, then composes his face into a studied neutrality again. His soldiers, whose hostility had slackened in the exchange of greetings, tighten their grips on the plastic guns they're sporting.

Theo: "Gotta take you in, y'all. You know the drill. Hands behind your backs. You're gonna meet the new president."

PETER

"SO WHAT'S YOUR STORY?" I ASK GUJA. He's stumping along the ashy-dark tunnel next to me.

"Story?"

"Yes. Where are you from, how did you get here, favorite band, so on and so forth."

He looks at me blankly at first, and I figure he doesn't know what I'm talking about, but he says, "Nepal."

"Oh," I say. Haven't really thought much about Nepal. "I thought you were from Britain."

He laughs. "No, we *fight* for Britain."

"Why's that? What did they ever do for you?"

He laughs again, a bright sound, almost a giggle, which seems out of keeping with his whole kill-on-command thing.

"They pay me," he says.

"So when this is all done, you going to move back to Nepal?"

"Maybe. Maybe I bring my family to England."

"Family?"

Another laugh, as though it were stupid to think anyone *wouldn't* have a family. "Wife, two girls, two boys."

"So . . . they're probably kind of worried about you."

He shrugs.

We walk on a bit farther. Then he says, "Coldplay."

"Excuse me?"

"Favorite band. Coldplay."

A chest-high platform opens up in front of us, and I realize that we're at the edge of the number 6 line, just a couple of levels down from Grand Central and the Bazaar. We've made it this far without seeing anybody, not even Mole People. Guess word of the massacre got around, and nobody thinks to hide down here anymore.

I turn to Titch. "It's best if I take a look-see first. No way can you pass for a kid up there. Sorry, gorgeous." I smile at Titch's beautifully battered heavyweight's face.

"Can't let you go alone, Peter," says Titch. "Can't risk the possibility of you scarpering, begging your pardon."

"Okay, I don't know what *scarpering* means, but I'm gonna guess that it's something like 'running away.'"

"That's about the size of it. If you're anything like Miss Zimmerman, you'll have a talent for buggering off without anybody's say-so."

"But we're gonna get about ten feet if I have a gigantic grown-up in tow."

"Take 'im, then." He means Guja. "He's got a baby face, in'e?"

I take a long look at Guja, and I decide that he could just about pass muster, given his height challenges.

"Fine. It's a deal. But he's got to lose some of the whole military look."

Guja removes his outer camo tunic, revealing a cute little undershirt. Now the rest of his equipment looks more like a fashion statement and less like professional gear. He keeps his weird knife, which frankly isn't much stranger than half the weapons you see kids carrying around anyhow.

"You go in, find out where the biscuit is, then come down and we figure out how to get it back. That, of course, will probably involve our skill set." He means himself and Guja. And he means killing.

"How many times have you been in the Bazaar?" asks Guja.

"Once or twice," I say breezily. Then, "Okay, once."

"Lovely," says Titch.

"It is," I say. "Nobody will recognize me." Though I'm not too sure even of that.

"All right," says Titch. "No faffin' about, right?"

"Yes. Whatever that means."

I turn and heave myself up onto the platform, and Guja follows. I realize, suddenly, that I'm in charge, instead of letting somebody else lead by default. It's weird because I've kind of gotten used to playing a secondary role. Like I believed all those movies in which it's always a white straight dude who's the hero. But now, it's, like, once you're past hierarchy, past perceived notions of who's supposed to do what, you get to lead by the power of your ideas.

But what *are* my ideas? Other than a vague notion of seeing Chapel again and either shooting him in the head or falling into his arms, I'm not sure. I guess saving the world from nuclear destruction ought to fit in there somewhere.

We travel up the stairways and corridors we fled down long ago, the scent of fresh air billowing from above, the armpit closeness of the underground giving way. The sound of humans gets louder and louder, like the garbled stew of words at a party when the speakers have blown out and the talk surges.

I'm remembering the first time—the only time—we came to the Bazaar. We were hoping to restock on ammunition and food. It was a full-on entrepreneurial jamboree occupying several levels of the old Grand Central train terminal, with hundreds of stalls and stores and bars and restaurants. That might imply something clean and orderly and hygienic, but it was more your teenage Mad Max gallows-humor riff on all of those things, with establishments like Slay Mart and Snack Food Glory Hole.

I *loved* it.

Didn't feel like leaving. The place seemed perfect. But there was a hitch. The place was controlled by the bank. And the bank was controlled by the Uptowners.

Anyway, the one good thing you could say about *them*, I mean if you were inclined to do that sort of thing, is that they were pretty big on law and order. So I'm surprised when we climb to the lower level of the Bazaar. There's no skinhead in camouflage guarding the subway exit like I remember from before. Maybe all available ex-lacrosse-player rapists are off fighting Wakefield and his squad.

But then I see the dead bodies, just sort of abandoned there on the tiles of the food court. Now, the Uptowners weren't sentimental or reverential of human life or anything, but they knew that rotting corpses weren't good for business. Moving around the bodies, there's a manic, gyrating crowd. Something's definitely up.

Stallkeepers scan the crowd warily. A kid grabs something, runs, and gets a crossbow bolt in the back. A necklace of Mardi Gras beads spills out of his hand, and he wheezes out his last breath. People just walk past him, over him.

You wouldn't have said it was exactly *civilized* the last time we were here, but it all made a kind of sense. It was all about *getting and spending*, as my homeboy Willy Wordsworth put it.

Now, though, it feels like there's a tumult beyond immediate desires. A buzzing restlessness, aimlessness, madness in the eyes of the people around us.

Beside me, Guja coughs from the diesel-scented air, and I turn to see him gawking at the high arched ceiling. He takes in Kentucky Fried Rat, International House of Handjobs, the Junkie Monkey. Rent boys and rent girls and armed pimps cruise the crowd; hundreds of household lamps, half of them dead, hang from the walls and from ropes strung along the ceiling. Eateries and bars spill out of the bounds of the old doughnut concessions and coffee chains. The stench of diesel and rotting flesh, the avid, predatory roaches, the braying teens. A look of deep unrest suffuses his face and grips his body, like I once saw on this kid who took too many mushrooms.

Me: "Hey. *Hey.* Keep it together." I figure his brain is reaching full culture shock and he needs a bit of a reminder. "Think of Cold-play or some shit."

He nods, seems to regather his identity.

But the crowd is getting more out of control, and it sweeps us up in its mass, threatening to disperse us like grains of sugar in hot water. We're dragged toward the makeshift boxing ring at the center of the echoing hall, where back in the day, poor SeeThrough and Jefferson fought a pair of crazy white boys for money.

No sign of Chapel, Wakefield, or the football. There's some sort of sales pitch going on. A kid wears a kind of parody of mid-level-salesguy clothes—collared shirt, khakis, lace-ups, all spattered with old grime and blood. At his side, a couple of Uptowner goons glower down on the crowd. The guy has a battery-powered loudspeaker that he's using to deliver his pitch.

"Now you may be asking yourself, *Self, how can we know that this is the real deal? The real, US Grade A Fancy, top-of-the-line, uncut Cure?* Well, I can vouch for it myself!"

He pats a big glass jug propped on a barstool, and the dark liquid inside sloshes back and forth a little. Kids in the crowd, worried that it'll tip over, gasp, and some of them try to make their way inside the ring. The guards in camouflage kick them off the ropes and wave guns around, promising death to the next person who climbs up uninvited.

"That's right!" shouts the salesguy. "Want to know how old I am, kiddos? I'll tell you. I'm twenty years old next week! And I've never felt better!"

Maybe he's telling the truth. It's hard to judge from his appearance, since the rigors of surviving in this place can make anybody look a little haggard. But what he's selling sure doesn't look like the stuff Brainbox and the Old Man cooked up.

The guy in the ring continues, "So you're probably wondering what kind of price we put on this Cure. What kind of price can you put on life itself? How about *twenty dollars*? Is that a good enough deal for you? They used to say that life was cheap to the Uptowners—I guess it's true!"

The salesguy basks in the rapture of the crowd. He's suddenly the center of a sea anemone of hands holding bank-approved twenty-dollar bills. The guards start helping kids up one by one, and the salesguy takes their money, still working the crowd.

He starts going all Oprah. "*You* get a life! And *you* get a life! And YOU get a life!"

"Life" comes in the form of a swig of the "Cure," administered from a dirty plastic Hello Kitty cup dipped into the jug. They drink, they faint in relief, they scream in exultation.

And the name Bugs Meany suddenly jumps into my head. You remember? In the Encyclopedia Brown books? Bugs Meany and his gang of older kids, the Tigers, were always ripping off the younger kids with bogus schemes. Then Encyclopedia would catch them in a lie and they'd have to confess.

This is kind of like that, except if you caught these boys in a lie, they'd just shoot you in the head.

All of a sudden, there's a commotion from the far side of the hall. I can see a handmade banner mounted on a pole above a mosh-pit-like disturbance in the crowd. Pictured on the banner is what at first looks like some kind of mutated human with extra limbs, or maybe a Hindu deity. But when the jostling under the banner stops for a moment, I see that it's a home-brew version of that Leonardo drawing, the one with the naked dude stretching his limbs out inside a circle. The banner jounces along as whoever is carrying it shoves their way through the crowd toward the boxing ring.

"Peter, what this is?" asks Guja, looking nervous.

"Hell if I know, G."

The man on the banner, like the Leonardo drawing, reminds me of pictures of Jesus on the cross, at least because his arms are spread out, and as the banner drifts closer, I can make out the drawing of the face more clearly. It's stylized, with almond-shaped eyes and black hair, and the man's expression is remarkably calm. At the top of the banner, someone's painted a big red *J*. Maybe the *J* does mean Jesus?

Turns out, it doesn't.

Things get weird fast.

"Repent! Repent!" a voice calls from beneath the weird square banner.

The huckster selling the fake Cure turns to look, confused, and the Uptowner guards point their guns. But I notice a couple of kids in ragged robes slip under the bottom ropes of the ring and sneak up behind the guards, who I guess don't hear them because of all the noise. Before the guards can fire, the robed kids pull knives out of their belts and, without warning, stab the guards and take their weapons.

Now others boil up over the edges, their faces wild, their heads stubbled and scabby. They carefully pass the banner hand over hand to the ring and set it up in the middle of the canvas floor. Then they smash the jug of "Cure" to the floor.

The suit-coated salesman, meanwhile, has melted into the crowd, making a run for it. The crowd turns ugly—they're furious that the promise of life has been taken away from them. A dude jostles me as he heads toward the boxing ring, shouting for blood.

"Repent!" says the leader of this strange new clique, which now definitely has the attention of the crowd.

In another place, at another time, two people being knifed to death would produce a panicked stampede, but here it's nothing new. The guards' blood flows toward the edge of the ring, where a little of the liquid dribbles down to the tile floor. Some kids open their mouths then lick up the Cure, or what they think is the Cure.

"Repent!" says the leader again, whose cray-looking face, with its mottled skin, stubble, and spiky eyebrows, looks weirdly familiar. "There is only one Cure!"

He holds up a yellow nylon rope, dark and discolored at the center of its length. "There is only one way out of the wilderness of the Sickness and into the paradise of New Life!" He says it like that, like some of the words are capitalized.

The kid parades around with his relic, holding it up for the crowd.

"You will not have New Life unless you touch the blood of *Jefferson*!"

And his companions shout, *"Jefferson!"*

There's this part in this movie I saw called *Jaws*. When the cop guy has just opened the beach, and he suddenly realizes there's a shark cruising around in the water selecting its next meal, and it looks like Roy Scheider is hurtling toward us, even though he's in the same place. Anyhow, that is how I feel right now—like I'm rushing toward this realization.

The *J* on the banner is for Jefferson. *Our* Jefferson. And the guy on the drawing with his quadruple legs and arms stretched out like that Leonardo drawing? That's him, too. Somebody has made a religion out of Jefferson. Or at least, they've taken facts—that we manufactured the Cure out of his blood, and that it works—and turned them into some kind of crazy-ass magical thinking.

That's where the rope comes in. And where it gets even stranger.

Because I realize it's the Ghosts. Or at least, they *were* the Ghosts, the insane cannibalistic cultists who we found living in the public library when we were searching for the Cure.

Back then, they were into a twisted version of the sacrament—wine turning to blood, bread turning to flesh. It was the way they justified eating people. They tried to convert us by forcing us to eat a meal with them. We wouldn't. They insisted. People died.

And on our way out, some of Jefferson's blood must have gotten onto the ropes they tied us with. Or maybe it's not even his blood. It could have been anybody's. Really, it doesn't matter. Anyway, that's what they're displaying to the crowd, like it's magic or something.

The Ghost continues, "I speak to you not as one of the elect but as a sinner, a sinner among sinners!" he shouts. "For he walked among us! But we did not understand! He came to bring us life! But we offered him death! We deserve nothing of him! But I have touched his holy blood—and so I *live*!"

He thrusts the nylon rope with the old blood on it into the air once again. I doubt the crowd knows what it all means, but something about the certitude of the gesture seems to convince them. They start to walk toward it, like metal filings drawn to a magnet.

Meanwhile, me? I'm backing away, with Gooj at my side. But—true confession? There's a little, eensy bit of me that is envious of Jefferson. I mean, brother never seemed to *care* about being famous. Me? I always wanted to be. And now *he's* the one with the profile.

But that doesn't last long. As the people rush the stage, me and Guja resist the push, becoming a sort of boulder blocking the stream of the crowd. It draws the attention of the dude with the rope. He turns to look at us—and sees me.

Now I guess if Jefferson is their new Big J, that makes *me* Saint Peter, which is to say, to them I'm Kind of a Big Deal, too.

I back away as the Ghost's face starts to wear a look that is maybe religious ecstasy but also a lot like a thirteen-year-old girl who just found herself in the presence of a member of One Direction. For a moment, he looks too surprised to do or say anything. Then he rushes to the edge of the ring, strains his body over the ropes, and thrusts the nylon cord toward me.

"Peter!" he shouts. "Peter! We have kept the faith! Save us! Take us to Jefferson!" The other Ghosts around him are starting to get wind of what's happening and floating toward the edge of the ring.

I don't know, in normal circumstances—if "normal circumstances" could ever be said to be the case up in this mofo—how I would react to being proclaimed the apostle of a new religion. I'd like to think that I'd take it pretty well. I'd let them down gently, at least. But this is probably the worst imaginable time to be recognized, even if the context is kinda flattering.

"I think we should go," I say to Guja.

"Copy that," he says. We turn and start to leave, but the cultists are not done with me.

"Peter!" they cry. "Stay! Stop him! Stop him!"

Now the faces of people in the crowd are turning toward us; I'm breathing fame on them like an airborne virus. Hands reach out to grab me.

It is at that moment that the Uptowner soldiers appear, rushing down from the ramps of the upper level, rifles up.

But they haven't come for me; they've come for the Ghosts who interfered in their sale of the fake Cure. The salesman points out the offenders, and the guards fire into the ring. A cultist to the right of the leader falls, and then the crowd finally recoils as bullets fly. It's like a shaken snow globe, a stampede, a gyrating mosh, and the distinction of being a saint is wiped away in the panic. When kids look at me now, it's only as another animal in their way as everyone tries to escape from the cross fire.

A figure falls to the ground in front of me. I make to step over it, but then I realize it's Guja. As he looks at me, wild-eyed, I pull him up and start dragging him toward the side ramp that leads up to the station's main concourse, away from the riptides of fleeing kids. He gets his feet under him, and we make it to the ramp heading up.

Gunfire and bloodshed are everyday here, and the crowd's panic simmers down the higher we go. The shouts and screams get hushed by the twists and turns of the granite corridors.

"What do those people want?" says Guja, once it feels safe enough to talk again.

"Who, them?" I say, kind of playing it off.

"They see you, and they go crazy."

"Oh, you know, it's just my personal magnetism. Ain't no thing."

I remind myself to stay Down to Earth.

Back before What Happened, when there was such a thing as celebrity, we used to joke about the phrase *down to earth*. People who met celebrities always called them that. *They're* so *down to earth*. I felt like this was due entirely to efforts on the part of the famous person to *seem* like it. And if you knew them in real life, you'd realize how fame had totally warped their personalities. You know. Your Kardashians. Your Trumps.

At least, that's how it felt back at the UN, when we were dispensing the Cure. Everyone was aware that, on some level, they couldn't live without Jefferson. After all, their lives were saved by a vaccine made from his blood. So they treated him with exaggerated respect and attention. Everything he said seemed to be in a larger font than everybody else's words, and everyplace he went seemed to be more interesting to them than it had been a moment before. It was messed up, and so is being idolized by a bunch of recovering cannibals, but still.

I'll admit it: There's a kind of skip in my step.

As we hit the main floor of the terminal, with its high, latticed windows and star-dappled ceiling, we dissolve into a new crowd, unaware of the shitstorm below. Up here, there's more businesses selling the Cure in every form—from pills to powders to injections. It's all got to be fake. The only real Cure I know is a batch they whipped up on the *Ronald Reagan* according to Brainbox's recipe and put in little sealed plastic packets that looked like doses of fast-food ketchup.

There was enough to treat the attendees of the Gathering at the UN, but that was it. For the rest, the plan was to fire up a lab— something that couldn't be done without a whole heap of resources and logistics and whatnot. Brainbox said he'd need a location, a staff, and, like, resources to make the stuff, and New York had been stripped clean of anything useful. I'm guessing that when everything went south at the Gathering, somebody made off with the remaining doses of the Cure—that, or it was lying scattered on the floor of the Security Council chamber.

Anyway, it's pretty unlikely that somebody has taken up the plan to manufacture more. Brainbox was probably the singularly most qualified kid to do it, and he's dead. And Chapel seems pretty uninterested in anything other than the biscuit.

He certainly doesn't seem interested in me.

"Hey, Guja," I say.

"Yes, Peter."

"When they were gearing you guys up for this mission, did they mention bringing any medicine? For the kids?"

Guja looks confused. Then he just smiles and shrugs, sort of like he's saying *Above my pay grade* or whatever. But I figure he'd know if they were gonna help us out, right? It's not exactly like they're distributing infected blankets, but this is no mercy mission, either.

Under the circumstances, I guess it's not surprising that there's a huge demand. Or that the market is meeting that demand with snake oil.

They're still selling other stuff, too, still issuing authorized money at the old ornately grilled ticket windows. But I can tell the camo-wearing Uptowner soldiers are spread thin. Here and there, you can see an item exchanged for another without the intervention of cash, which never would've been allowed before. Now handshakes and private understandings get around the rules of the Uptowners.

Up the staircase under the cracked Apple Store altar, a boy with a hoarse voice shouts a speech about the treachery of barter and credit. And below, in the horseshoe-shaped whirlpool of stalls, Uptowner soldiers pull violators away and summarily execute them, staining the marble walls with blood.

"Crazy," says Guja. "Crazy people." His hand reaches to touch his knife for reassurance.

"Yeah," I say. "They're slippin'."

In theory, I ought to be happy, since it looks like Evan and his thugs are losing their hold. But all it means for now is that things are more dangerous than they ever were. Like, if there's one thing worse than a police state, it's a failing police state, with the rulers grabbing desperately at their power and strivers rushing in to pick up the pieces. That dude Evan must be trippin'. I mean, more than usual.

The Gathering was supposed to stop all this from happening. The Bazaar was going to be peaceful, a neutral territory, maintained by a multitribe security force. At least, that's what Chapel and Jefferson said.

"Look," says Guja. He points with his chin toward the opposite end of the Grand Concourse, where a squad of camo'ed Uptowners is forcing its way through the crowd.

They have Wakefield and one of the other Gurkhas on rope leads, urging them forward with blows. Wakefield looks around, dazed, too battered to orient himself. The Gurkha keeps his head down, absorbing the punches and slaps stoically.

"Kulbir," says Guja to himself, or something that sounds like it anyway.

"Chill," I say to Guja, who looks like he's fixing to take some heads. "We follow."

IMANI

THEY'RE BACK AGAIN. Those white kids.

Now, before you get all offended, let me explain. I'm not a racist. See, racism is a matter of a *system*. To be a racist, you have to be the party in control, and we are not. Yes, we have control over our own litlle dominion from 110th up to 135th, Saint Nicholas East to the FDR. But we are an island in a sea of the Other. And though the structures of power have been toppled, the ruins are still clogging shit up.

When I say I am not happy to see these kids walk into my office in the old brownstone on MLK, understand then that it is because they in general and *they* in particular have never had our best interests in mind and have done *nothing* on our behalf.

Spider? Dead. Captain? Gone. Theo says it was by his own choosing, and may Allah, the compassionate, the merciful, watch over him. As for Theo, those fools kept him chained up so he couldn't reveal the truth—that we weren't alone in the world.

You're gonna say that blond bitch saved Theo's life. Yes, but that was a side effect, not her intention. And I know Theo has a soft spot for her. But brothers have been falling for milky-skinned, yellow-haired hos for four hundred years now, on account of the poison that has been poured into their brains by the media. Doesn't mean she's worth the DNA she's encoded in.

But here she is, with two other little blond kids, straight-up little Aryan crackers, and that boy Jefferson, who last time I saw him was debating me at the Apollo, right before he broke his word to us and spread the Cure around to anybody who asked, like it was Halloween candy. Well, I was here in this very room when he told Solon that only Harlem and their tribe would get the Cure, if we would help him get to Plum Island. Solon was sitting where I am now. Me, I was in the corner, doing my Dick Cheney shit.

So we sent Spider and Captain and Theo in the ship, all the way to the end of Strong Island, and two of them didn't come back. And at his "Gathering," our enemies—otherwise known as everybody else—got rewarded just the same as us.

Well, Solon is gone, and I'm in charge of Harlem now. And

Jefferson doesn't look so high-and-mighty, not like when he was selling his line about peace and love and life, bullshitting the brothers and sisters, telling them we all, in the words of the old secular hymn, could get along. We have heard this again and again. It is our nature to fall for this because we are a loving people, because we are a generous people.

No, Jefferson looks hollow, he looks beat, and I'm glad. He lied and turned my peeps against me, and now he can barely look me in the eye. It's a strange thing that the eye, just an organ of perception after all, should have a moral force, a repulsive charge like a magnet pointed the wrong way, when you've done wrong. That's how Mama always knew I was lying: when I couldn't meet the power of her gaze. And when she knew, she beat me. And her beatings gave me strength in time, when I understood that she did it to save me from an even worse fate, if I were not constantly aware of every crosscurrent of danger pulsing through a white man's world.

So Jefferson is quiet now, his head down, his body still, like if he didn't exert any energy he'd be invisible. Like I'm a T. rex that only sees motion. Instead, it's Donna, the little raggedy-ass one, giving the line this time.

It goes like this: They're selling slaves down at the museum on the west side of the park. Your people were in bondage once. So you should help us free *our* people.

And I say to her, "Oh, *now* you're against slavery."

And she says, "Of course. I've *always* been against slavery. I'm against murder, too."

So I say to her, "Well, if that's the case, what did you ever do about it?"

And she says, "What do you mean? Slavery was over by the time I was born."

"Actually," says the fine-ass Indian-but-English-sounding dude who's new to the whole scenario, and a welcome addition, I may add, "that's not true. We still have slavery down in the Subcontinent; they just don't call it that."

"Well, not *here*," Donna says.

"And you think you have nothing to do with slavery?" I say. "You have nothing to do with the past? You don't have to have committed a crime to be *part* of it."

Pretty much blank stares.

I pick up an apple from the bowl on my desk, one of the good ones we get from the farmers up in Strong Island. I push the bowl their way, as if to say, even though you're out of line, I still maintain certain standards of hospitality. They don't bite. They're not hungry, on account of they probably think I'm gonna have them executed.

I say, "Let me put it to you this way. If something's been stolen, and you end up with it, what should you do? I mean, if you

didn't do anything to get it, it just fell in your lap? Let's say...
okay. Let's say your great-grandma had a gold ring stolen by the
Nazis. Right?"

Donna is following so far.

I continue, "Well, it passes on down the line, until sixty years
later some girl who didn't have anything to do with World War
Two, never gave the Nazi salute, wouldn't hurt a fly, gets that
ring for a present. Now, when she finds out it belonged to your
grandma. What should she do?"

Donna thinks. I'll give her credit—she's already almost
there. She says, "She should give me the ring back. It wasn't
hers in the first place. It wasn't her family's to give."

"That's right," I say. "So. *Where is the labor of my ancestors?*"

I pause because they don't have an answer; then I continue, "The fortunes they built. The houses. The roads. The
mills. The industry. The *country* my ancestors built. The one
you got to live it up in, with police to protect you from all the
great-great-great-grandchildren like me nobody knew what to
do with. When do you give us back what we made and you took
from us? And you know what? We weren't even asking for all of
it. Just a little piece of God's green earth where we could live
and get treated like human beings. See?"

She's nodding, like either she understands or she's just pretending to, trying to get my help. But Blondie, not so much.

"Well," says Blondie, "it's all over now. All that's in the past. We're all in the same boat now."

"That's right," I say. "It's a clean slate. Nobody owes anybody anything. Nome sane?"

"Imani," says Jefferson. He's staring down at the pattern on the Indian carpet.

Now, I don't really like that he can just say my name like that, like I was the same as anybody he knows, like any of my friends would say it.

"You can call me Madam President," I say.

"Okay. Madam President. If it's because of me...well, please don't keep from doing the right thing just because of me."

If I didn't think I was doing the right thing, I wouldn't be doing it. It's not like I'm refusing to help these fools just to spite them. But I let him go on. I'm a good listener. It helps me figure out how to beat people.

"I'm sorry," he says, "for everything. Maybe you were right. Maybe you should have just kept the Cure and killed everybody else. Maybe you had the right."

Then he goes quiet. I don't see why I have to finish his thoughts for him.

"But?" I say.

He shrugs. Says nothing. Then, like that kind of thing probably doesn't matter anymore, he says, "Saving those girls is the right thing to do." Which he's already basically said.

So I say, "I don't see why nobody else has to do the 'right' thing and *I* do. Who are those girls to me? Somebody else's tribe, people I never met. And besides. Nobody ever knows what the right thing is until it's too late to decide, do they?"

So I start thinking. I mean, I'm always thinking; Mama said I was thinking since the moment I came into the world. But now I'm thinking. Deep, deep down inside me, trying to get to what the right thing really is.

The white kids don't know what to make of that. They look around at each other like they think I'm just done. It's all right. I've gotten used to how people react to me, when I go away for a little bit like this. If people actually took any time to just sit and *think* when they needed to, they wouldn't be surprised when they see me doing it.

"Well," says Jefferson, "I guess we better go."

"No," I say, "that's cool."

They shoot glances at each other. Look at their hands. They don't know what I mean.

I say, "I'm not going to do it because it's the 'right thing.' I'm going to do it because it feels good."

What I mean is, I'm going to help them. I'm going to get my girls together and send them to rain hell on those slavers. I won't do it because it's right, or for Washington Square, or because of the past.

I'll do it to see those little fuckers piss in their pants. I'll do it to make the Uptowners' hair stand up on their necks because they know we're coming for them next. I'll do it to see the looks in the girls' eyes when they realize they've been freed.

I'll do it for me.

We're taking five of the pickups to the slave market. My girls are in the beds, fifty in all, each with a 3-D–printed AR-15 in her hands. We come prepared.

"So what do you call them?" asks Rab—that's his name. He means my girls.

"What, are you still talking to me?" I say. I can feel his arm rub up against mine as the truck jounces this way and that. I like it, but it makes me feel nervous. "You got what you wanted, didn't you?"

"Can't I talk to you?" says Rab, his head bouncing off the ceiling as I turn a corner.

The suspension is jarring, and there's not much room in the cab, but I don't mind. I'm not in the mood for a long walk, especially since I can imagine a *few* situations in which we will want to get out quickly.

"Why don't you talk to your skinny little girlfriend?" I say. I've clocked the way he looks at Donna. They're not together but they have been, is my opinion. She's hiding it from Jefferson, who is starting to get it. But what do I know? I'm not exactly the mistress of romance or anything. I decide to answer his question anyway. "My girls call themselves the Slayer Queens," I say. "Now let me concentrate on driving."

But actually, I kind of like the way he talks, all fancy and British and everything. Outside, I'm mean-mugging, but inside, I'm like, *Say more things!*

I ask him, "You ever hear of Rojava?"

He shakes his head.

I tell him about how the Kurds—that's these people up in the Middle East that never had a home—like, they're beefing with the Turks, they're beefing with the Syrians, they're beefing with the Iraqis, nobody wants to let them have their own little piece of the earth. Everyone tells them to just shut up and move along.

"I've heard about the Kurds," says Rab, only he pronounces it "kuuuuuuuds." "But I'm not sure how they fit in here."

"If you let me finish, you'd know," I say, and I can't help but feel like I'm flirting maybe just a little bit. I say, "They started this tiny country called Rojava, in a sliver of land up in the north of Syria, when everything started going to shit there, Assad and ISIS and all. They based their government on these books some old dude who everybody had forgot about wrote—this old professor who thought he was finished, just lying on the couch all day nursing his joints in some run-down cottage in Maine. Well, one day old dude gets an e-mail from somebody who says he's the imprisoned Kurdish leader, who tells him, we've decided to adopt your political ideas for this new country we're starting. Imagine that. Folks halfway around the world who think he's the best thing since Karl Marx."

"Intriguing," says Rab.

"Anyway," I say, "the idea is total equality, between races, between religions, between genders. Every government position has one man and one woman in it. Every cop has to go to two weeks of feminist training before he can put on the badge. They even have a brigade of female fighters, and the ISIS *Kuffars* are shit scared of them because they think that they can't go to heaven if they're killed by a woman.

"So when Solon lost his mandate and I got the presidency, I decided to emulate the Kurds and put together a little all-girl force of our own. People want to take a shot at us, let them come."

Rab nods. He says, "I like a strong woman." I take a look at him as he watches the road.

We move along MLK, past Marcus Garvey, down Malcolm X. Right on 110th, across the top of the park, the slick of Harlem Meer reflecting the sickly winter sun. Mean mugs. Shiny guns.

Slavers, my girls coming for you.

PETER

WHEN THEY DRAG WAKEFIELD AND THE other Gurkha dude in, my homey Guja and me are watching from a sort of crawl space above a big disused restaurant set in the vaulted guts of the station. Gooj scoped it out—behind an access door marked MAINTENANCE ONLY. Turns out he's an infrastructure geek, has plans to be a building inspector once he's finished decapitating people. Below us, through a metal grating with little holes that look like stylized flower petals, I can see a U-shaped counter topped with white Formica, strangely cafeteria-like amid the churchy formality of the oily redbrick walls. It's some kind of board meeting of the Uptown Confederacy. These boys are nasty pieces of work from the various private schools that dotted the Upper East Side.

Among them, I recognize Evan immediately, his hair as blond and his cheekbones as high as ever. Observing him unnoticed from up here, without the distraction of his trying to kill me or vice versa, I consider him abstractly for the first time. *Abstractly*, he's every bit as good-looking as his sister. They both have that Nordic, WASPy thing going on.

But he's strangely unsexy. Oh, it's not just that he's a psychopath and murderer. I mean, when has that ever stopped anybody from finding somebody hot? All those serial killers who got girlfriends through the mail?

There's something about Evan, though—it's like your libido just bounces off the surface of his handsomeness. The Bad Boy appeal goes only so far until it curdles into something off-putting. In fact, his classical features are part of what makes him downright repulsive. The contrast between appearance and reality is too perverse; he's a flower growing out of shit.

And then in walks Chapel.

When we first met, I was in the brig of the *Ronald Reagan*, slowly going crazy from isolation. He appeared like a dream in the middle of the night and laid out the state of the world, at least as he wanted me to understand it. I learned that the rest of the globe had survived the Sickness and was held together with spit and glue and constant surveillance and the United States Navy. Chapel said he was from a group that called themselves the Resistance, which aimed to free humanity from the yoke of global tyranny and stuff.

But there was more. Or at least, I thought so. An affinity...an attraction. After a while, Chapel visited me for reasons other than political instruction.

I thought I was in love. I was ready to follow him anyplace.

And I guess I did follow him anyplace, given that I'm bent over in a crawl space in Grand Central. Rats be going by like, *What are you doing here?* Guja backs away, like he might have signed up for combat but not *rodents*.

While I fell for Chapel, Jefferson, of course, fell for Chapel's con. He told us about the Reconstruction Committee's plot to let all the surviving kids in the US die off before moving in to, as Chapel vividly put it, *scrape off the goo and restart the factories.*

So when he claimed he wanted to Save the Children, we were all on board, and we worked to get back to the last place I wanted to go—New York.

As for what Chapel wants *now*, or what he really wanted in the first place, who knows. Maybe he actually does want to Fight the Power. Maybe he just wants to Be the Power. Either way, since he's got the biscuit, in theory he can pretty much do what he likes, on account of anytime he wants he can blow up the world.

This is, of course, a much, *much* bigger issue than the fact that he took off without saying good-bye. But you know, human nature is what it is, so the very personal experience of dumpage somehow manages to outweigh the geopolitics for me. I'm ashamed to say it *almost* feels as present to me as the fact that he shot Brainbox. Damn. Can't even get my head around *that* yet.

Regardless, right now Chapel is surrounded by brutal, heavily armed ex-private-school boys. I can't imagine Evan is going to be content with entourage status and just let somebody else run the world, so there's a reasonable chance that Chapel's going to end up with his throat cut. Which I guess would be satisfying in a that's-what-you-get-for-what-you-did kind of way, except that the only thing worse than Chapel with his finger on the button is Evan with his finger on the button. I have, like, minimal respect for that kid's good sense. Him and his sister both.

"Look, Peter," Guja's whispering urgently.

Wakefield and the Gurkha are shoved through the doors of the Oyster Bar and down to their knees in front of Chapel, Evan, and the Uptowner bigwigs. Something about the curve of the high ceiling makes it easy to hear the conversation that follows.

EVAN

CHAPEL WON'T LET ME HOLD THE COOKIE or the biscuit or whatever, which is fucking lame of him. Like he thinks I'm going to fiddle around with it and launch a bunch of nuclear missiles by accident or something. Like I'm a five-year-old. Like he's Dad, so he gets to hold the remote.

I guess I can't figure out a particularly good reason why I *need* to hold it at the moment, other than that I want to, and that Chapel doesn't want me to. It's the old "want" and "need" thing again. I remember my father dadsplaining it to me in that particularly smug way that made me want to smash his teeth in with a hammer.

Dad liked to claim that most of what we think we *need* is actually what we *want*—this was usually because I told him I needed a car, or some cool shoes, or whatever. He even said that human wants were limitless. Like, once you had something you thought you needed, which really was just something you wanted, you always found something else to want, even if, in the end, what you wanted most was more time on earth.

One day, I thought I had him because I said I could think of a need, which was air, and then he said, *Well, could you think of a situation in which you might be willing to sacrifice your life for something?* And I thought, *Absolutely not.*

But I wanted to seem like a "good person," so I said yes, and he said, *Ah, you see? You didn't actually need air in that case because you put something else you wanted ahead of it. In fact, you'll find that when it comes down to it, there is no such thing as a need at all.*

Which was kind of his assholish way of saying I wasn't going to get the convertible for weekends out in the Hamptons, which was totally unfair. He was really difficult to argue with at times like this, so I waited until I had a good comeback.

It was a few weeks into What Happened, after the Internet had gone down, and the doctors and the nurses had left, and the cook and the maids had quit. Dad had caught the Sickness and Mom was avoiding him like the plague (ha-ha), and he was stuck in his filthy bed in his huge bedroom upstairs.

I entered his room after knocking softly, like he'd want me to, and I walked over to his bed and sat by his side and smiled. He wasn't used to my giving a shit about him, so I think he was really touched, even though he couldn't speak by that point.

Dad, I want you to know that, no matter what happens, I will always remember you, and everything you've told me over the years.

A glimmer in his eyes. He could hear me.

Like, remember that time you told me that you didn't need air?
Confusion.

Then I put my hand over his mouth and pinched his nose shut. I know that the traditional method is with a pillow, but if you do it that way, you don't get to see their face as they're dying.

I thought about DNA, and how I was cutting short the particular strain that had led to me. A phrase ran through my mind: *destroying the evidence.*

Then I thought about whether killing him wasn't actually merciful, since he already had the Sickness, and that was almost enough to make me take my hands away. But by then I was too busy making my point, and I didn't want to show weakness. Dad had always tried to beat and harass weakness out of me. So maybe in some way he was proud, you know, of his decisive son, who stayed the course. But he didn't look proud. He looked frightened.

I suppose, Dad, you could say I don't need *to do this. I just really want to.*

That was the last thing he heard, the last thing his brain processed before he stopped and then I stopped.

I went out and told Sis. She called me a monster. But she looked grateful to me for the first time in her life.

I wondered if it mattered that, after all he had done to me and Sis, his last thoughts were of defeat and betrayal and humiliation. Or was the fact that he was now dead the more important thing—that everything, all his memories, were wiped from the universe—and how it had ended was irrelevant?

Of course, *I* was here, and alive, and that was what really mattered, and I would carry inside me the beautiful memory of his ultimate destruction.

But I digress.

Dad's socioeconomic theories aside, I have worked a lot in my short life at distinguishing *want* from *need*—there were a lot of sessions with clever Jewboy Dr. Klein where we talked about nothing but that—so I'm pretty evolved. Back in the day, I might have just blasted Chapel and kept the biscuit, but I realize that this may not be in my long-term interest. I do make a little mental note to add this to my Reasons That I Am Going to Put a Bullet in Chapel's Head at Some Point Down the Line, but for now, I just hand it back to him with a smile.

Let me do the talking, he says.

Another reason added to the list.

Then they bring in the prisoners, a tall, old white guy and a scrappy, little brown guy in military gear. My bros sit up and ooh and aah. At some point, I guess we'll get used to seeing old people again but not yet. They look freakish, all crow's-feet and patches of sickly gray hair.

The hell are you? I say. I'm not going to leave all the talking to

Chapel. He looks at me sidelong. Neither of the prisoners says anything, but I catch them looking at the fat black briefcase by my chair and the biscuit in Chapel's hands.

British special forces, says Chapel, *judging by their uniforms.* He says it in a way like, *I know what I'm doing and you don't, so step off.*

What are "British special forces" doing here? I ask him.

Chapel looks annoyed, as if he doesn't want me to show our hand by revealing what we don't know, or something. But the way I figure it, we're the guys with the guns and they're the guys with their hands zip-tied behind their backs, so it can't really hurt to cut to the chase. I'm showing them that they are totally in my control by not holding my cards close to my chest. Like, *Look all you want because this is only gonna end with my boot on your neck anyway.*

Still not a peep from the oldsters.

As I told you, says Chapel, *the American Reconstruction Committee is centered in the UK.*

So why didn't they send some ass-kickers from the US to find the football, once they knew it had been located?

Then I figure it out. Because to get the job done, you might have to kill some folks, and it's much easier to kill foreigners than your own people, right? Because the lives of foreign people aren't worth as much. That's why in the news when there was an accident or something, it would always go, like, *One hundred twenty-six people feared dead, twelve Americans on board,* because American people put a different value on American lives. And British people put a different value on British lives, and Tanzanian people put a different value on Tanzanian lives. It's natural. That's why we found it so easy to bomb the shit out of other countries—because foreign kids mattered, like, some fractional amount of our own kids because they were far away and they looked different.

Anyhow, it stands to reason that if you wanted to go kick ass and take names here in the Big Apple, you would send some dudes who didn't feel particularly upset about killing the locals, like a bunch of limeys and other foreign types.

They think they can treat us like we're not from the first world or something. This makes me angry, and they're not saying boo in response to my questions anyway, so I make a snap decision, raise my AR-15, and—*BrrrAAAAP*—put a few bullets into the little brown guy.

He falls backward, and since he and the other dude have been tied together, it drags *him* backward, too, and what with the noise and the smell of gunshots, there's quite a commotion.

Chapel looks at me like I'm crazy, which is good, because I want him to think that. Like, best to remind him that he is in *my* house and he should ask before going into the fridge.

My guys snip the bonds between the now-dead little guy and the now-freaked-out big guy. I bet he has had some kind of antitorture training or whatever, but that would help you if you were dealing with rational people. Whereas he is dealing with me.

He looks, to say the least, wrong-footed.

Now I know we're on the same page. This way, there's no need to shout (a) because it's suddenly very, very quiet and (b) because, you know, when you kill somebody, you kinda have the floor anyways.

I'd just like to clear the air, get to the point, that sort of thing, I say. *By now it's probably obvious that we have the biscuit, and I figure you're looking for it. Am I right?*

I look at the guy, and he nods, almost automatically, before his better instincts have the chance to override his survival instinct (which, if you ask me, is the *best* instinct there is).

The other dudes you were with, that was all the people who they sent, right?

Wakefield says, *Support staff, back in the park.*

That's right, I say. *Zeke?* I call out to one of my best bros. *Go peep on them, right, see what they're up to?*

Zeke nods and heads out, his shaggy hair flopping back and forth. I don't have loads of people to spare, what with the chaotic state of affairs that the arrival of the Grown-ups has brought, but this seems like a pretty good use of resources. I will not miss him if he gets erased.

I feel like we're finally getting places. Now my colleague Mr. Chapel will take over.

Chapel has now recovered some of his composure, which went out the window after I unfriended the little guy. He turns back from the aisle he's been pacing.

Not exactly military discipline, Colonel, says Chapel. *I apologize. I think it should be obvious that we both find ourselves a little out of our comfort zone.*

The British guy gives Chapel a look like he's not having any of this attempt at a bonding moment. Like, the whole good cop deal.

But, continues Chapel, *as you can see, I have fallen on the winning side of the equation for now.*

So it seems. Finally, the guy speaks, and like most people, he can only figure out how to act based on shit he saw on TV. Hence, the underplayed attitude, like he's been through this kind of thing before.

Name? asks Chapel.

Wakefield, the guy says.

Wakefield, there's a way that everybody can get out of this alive, with his skin and his dignity intact.

Except for Private Bahadur. The guy nods toward his dead buddy.

Yeah, says Chapel. *I would have advised against that. But we're dealing with a bit of a loose cannon. Is that unfair?*

He looks to me as he asks the question.

I'm the loosest cannon, baby, I say. *Looser than loose. I'm not just a bad cop, I'm the worst cop.*

Chapel leaves it at that. *Now, you must have some sort of means of keeping in touch with the outside world? Sat comms? I could, of course, use this*—he indicates the biscuit—*but I'd rather not mess around with it, get me? To prevent any accidents.*

The guy says nothing. Then he looks at me and reaches his zip-tied hands toward one of many gear pockets on his cool-guy uniform. I nod to one of my guys, and he searches Wakefield and fetches out a little cell-phone thing with heavy rubber grips. Brings it to me. I decide to throw Chapel a bone, so I hand it on to him.

Access code? says Chapel. *And not the panic signal. It's in everybody's interest that we establish communications.*

Wakefield tells him a series of numbers and letters, which would be hard to guess, except, of course, pretty easy if you threaten to kill the guy who has it memorized. Torture is the ultimate hack.

Chapel enters the code, and somebody must pick up immediately, as if they've been waiting by the phone like a little bitch, because Chapel says, *No, this is Chapel, USN.* Which must mean "US Navy."

I'll wait, says Chapel.

Then I say to him, *Speakerphone, please.*

And Chapel looks at me like he doesn't want everybody to hear, and I look at him like I don't give a shit. Chapel thumbs a button on the satphone thing and sets it on the counter.

There's the sound of some shifting around on the other end. Then somebody says, *How did you get access to this line?*

I took it from your man Wakefield.

We need confirmation of that.

Chapel nods to Wakefield, who says, *This is Colonel Wakefield. I've been taken prisoner by*— He doesn't know who we are.

Uptown, bitches, I say.

There's a silence on the other end. Then, *What do you want?* Kind of weirdly personal, weirdly peevish, when I was expecting something official-sounding, or at least threatening.

I want a line through to the Reconstruction Committee, Chapel says. *And I want you to facilitate contact with the Resistance. I'll give you the necessary IP address in my next transmission. In the meantime, so that you know this is important, your man Wakefield here will confirm that I am in possession of the football and the biscuit. Stand by.*

And Chapel gets up and fetches the briefcase, opens its maw, riffles through some laminated pages of numerical codes. Then he holds up the biscuit, which is like a bigger version of what we're talking on.

Wakefield looks at it, stifles a gasp, and says, *I can confirm that.*

There's more silence on the other end. You can actually hear people *whispering* to each other. Pathetic.

Let me lay it out for you, says Chapel. *You're going to get the prime minister's office and the US embassy on the line. I'll wait one hour. I'll be in touch. If I don't get a response, I'll start warming up the missiles.*

Then he presses the Off button. Boop. Nuclear threat made.

It's not going to work, says Wakefield.

What's not going to work? says Chapel.

Whatever it is you have in mind.

Well, you'd better hope for your own sake it does. And for everyone's sake. He waggles the biscuit in his hand.

My boys take Wakefield away. He can chill at the bar next door. With his ankle manacled to the footrest.

Okay, so you boosted his cell phone. Why are we keeping him alive? I ask.

Because he's useful. He can validate what we say to the Reconstruction Committee.

He's like a—what do you call it—a certificate of authenticity.

Unless they think we've been torturing him. Chapel gives me a look.

If you can manage that. So don't mess him up, is what you're saying.

Like I'm some kind of sadist.

I go quiet for a while. Who does this guy think he is? He wouldn't be alive if I hadn't vouched for him. And here he is giving *me* orders. But *I'm* the one in charge here.

Okay, I say, *What now? I mean, what is your plan? Other than getting to meet famous people?*

The plan, he says, *is to begin negotiations with the Reconstruction Committee. That's a joint US-British authority that effectively runs the world. A little hard to explain the ins and outs to you, but*

I'm guessing you wouldn't go too far wrong if you just thought of a big version of parents.

I say, *I didn't get along very well with my parents, in the end.* He looks like he kind of wants to know what I mean, but kind of doesn't. *Why negotiate?*

Because, for one, they have a lot of my people in prison. They have to release them. Then they have to release the rest of the world.

My bros are watching the conversation like a tennis match, but if they didn't know the rules of tennis. Probably they're trying to figure out what's in it for them.

Sounds pretty communist to me, I say. In point of fact, I don't really know what *communist* means, but anything that sounds sort of namby-pamby seems to work. *And what does the Rest of the World do when it's released?*

In theory, whatever it wants. Opinions vary. Some of my associates think that a new era of peace and harmony will begin once the one percent are forced to reckon with their crimes. Myself, I think it'll be a global clusterfuck.

So why are you making it happen?

Chapel looks away, thinking. His expression is kind of hard to read. Like, maybe sad. But why is he doing it if it's such a bummer?

I suppose because something has to give, Evan.

I don't like being Mr. Question-Asking Guy, but I do have one more that I want answered. It's what the bros are thinking, and I'd prefer to stop them from thinking at all.

So where do we fit in? I say. *I mean to say, I don't really give a crap about your global justice or whatever.*

No. You are about the here and now.

That's all there is.

You're very Zen.

Never thought of it that way.

Well, Evan, the way you fit in is, you do what you do. I have the biscuit. I know how to use it. You have the men to guard it. From people like Wakefield. I don't think he'll be the last.

Let them come, I say. *But look, bro, I'm not exactly stoked to be the captain of the guards, you get me? Like you sitting on the throne and me . . .* What did they call it in Dad's office? *Reporting to you. I think* you *should report to me.* To emphasize the importance of this, I take my pistol out and twirl it around.

Chapel looks at me.

Fine, he says. *By the powers vested in me by the International Resistance, I hereby give you the rank of general and confer on you the political command of the plague zone. I humbly submit my résumé as advisor to Your Excellency.*

He thinks he's playing me, but I find these things end up counting for something. Your Excellency. I like the sound of that.

You're hired, I say.

But I think to myself, *Soon as I figure out how to work this biscuit thing, you're fired. I'ma go Trump on your ass.*

JEFFERSON

IT'S STRANGE TO BE IN a motor vehicle again. The Harlemite pickups move at impossible speed, hours of distance flying past in minutes. We approach the future too fast, a bloodbath sucking us toward itself before I can think my way around it.

This isn't the first time, of course, that presentiments of death have come up, and like before, I try to think of other things to keep my mind from shorting out. I look at the passing scenery, trying to identify things from their ruins. Pet groomer. Hair salon. Vitamin store. They seem to vibrate tinnily, echoes of life from long ago.

But among the reminders of the past, there are flashes of now. A kid turns the key of an opener on a can of dog food. A random runs after our trucks, asking us to take him along, but the girls bat him back. Dogs chase cats chase rats.

I have a new long gun, a boxy version of an AR-15 in fluorescent-pink plastic. It's from a special run made out of scrounged girl-focused LEGO kits. Imani's tribe melts them down and extrudes them into a fine plastic thread, which their Maker-Bot 3-D printers turn into gun housings. A separate crew fabricates the high-impact innards of the lower receiver from aluminum; yet another turns metal tubing into rifle barrels.

Yet another crew puts colorful stickers on. Unicorns vomiting rainbows, kittens giving thumbs-up.

We pull the trucks into a big, flat snow-covered space in a park on Seventy-Seventh and Amsterdam. We'll use the playground, whose structures look like wintry little castles in their mantles of snow and ice, for a staging area before the raid.

Imani sweeps the snow off the deck of a play structure and sets down the map. The residual snowmelt bleeds into the paper.

They found the blueprint at the public library, a while back when they were preparing to take over the entire island. That was before I brought the news of the Cure. When everyone realized that they could live for decades longer, their calculations of risk were thrown, and suddenly a Harlem blitzkrieg didn't seem worth it. But they had already, under Solon's diligent command, compiled an intelligence trove worthy of a proper invasion, including schematics of all the major tribal headquarters. One of those being, as it happens, the Museum of Natural History.

I wonder where Solon is now. Imani says he ran but not where. It sounds like he escaped, if she's telling the truth. I'm relieved, but I'm also afraid of having to explain myself to him someday. I thought it would be best that the tribes of New York would learn the truth like a frog in slowly heated water, but obviously that plan didn't work. And by the time the truth came out, in a single blast, Solon had staked his office and reputation and maybe his life to back me. I hope he's someplace peaceful, a stoic in retirement, like he wanted to be.

"There," says Theo, planting down his thick finger on the map. "That's the best way in."

He's pointing out a side door around the corner from the ornamental entrance portico. A narrow staircase to the first floor.

I say, "If this interior door is shut, we'll be stuck in this corridor."

"If the interior door is shut, I'm gonna make it Not Shut." He holds up a piece of gray putty—plastic explosive. "'Sides, it's not up to you."

Theo has been giving me a fairly frosty vibe all the way down. Not that I can blame him. The way he sees it, I left him in the hands of Resistance fighters on the east end of Long Island and took off for Manhattan. I didn't realize that they were about to kill him, though—luckily, Kath and the Thrill Kill Twins were there to spring him loose.

And I wonder if there isn't something else that makes him like me even less. Something about the way he looks at Kath. Something about the time they spent together. I remember that when they met, the first time we were in Harlem, she was convinced Theo was some kind of thug. But I guess they got to know each other pretty well, bushwhacking their way from the Hamptons back to the city with the twins, because she doesn't talk about him that way anymore.

And though I may have my own difficulties with Theo—he did, after all, nearly get me killed at the UN—I've always thought of him as solid, pensive, self-contained. Dangerous, but not to his friends. To tell the truth, I'm glad to have him in the fight. Imani didn't want him along, saying it was *a woman thing*, but Theo wouldn't have it.

"Theo's right," I say. I turn to Imani. "It's your show."

"All right, then," says Imani. "Three teams. One in front. You from the side. And the final team does their thing from above. We good?"

"We good," say the girls in one voice. The Slayer Queens (their term, not mine) are a formidable bunch, even with their Day-Glo equipment. Done up in everything from skirts to flak jackets, helmets and berets.

"Listen up," says Imani, and the girls go quiet. Steam trails up from fifty mouths.

"We go in strong. Anything got a beard, kill it. Anyone female, you get them out of there alive."

She looks around at her troops, her face set in a scowl.

"Now make 'em *feel you*."

We leave the pickups under guard and head to our rallying

points. Me, Kath, the twins, Theo, Donna, and Rab pass a bodega, restaurants, a pharmacy, a liquor store, and then cut over to Columbus, aiming to slip along the side of the museum out of view of the front.

Rab is looking down at a strange little letter-opener-looking thing in his hands.

"What's that?" I ask.

"Oh, this," he says. "A gift from my employers. It's a special sort of knife."

"Show me," I say. He hesitates, then hands it over.

It's a wickedly sharp little thing, triangular in cross section.

"Nice," I say. "But hopefully you won't get close enough to use it."

"You never know," he says.

"Better to use the pistol. Trust me."

"I haven't... This must make me seem *terribly* innocent to you, but I've never killed anyone. Never even tried."

"You'll manage," I say, "if you have to."

"I suppose," he says. The look in his eye is hard to read. "But how will I know if I have to?"

"Depends," I say. "Depends what you want."

"Yes," he says. Then, a little shyly, "Are you afraid? To die?"

The honest answer would be *Not as much as I used to be.* Because I have been in the middle realm, I have let go of my body, I have faced the *bardos* that test the soul's attachment. And the only thing that really tied me to the earth was Donna.

But that's too much of a mouthful, and besides, saying no might just sound like bragging.

So I say, "Yes. Of course. Who isn't?" And I give him back his knife.

PETER

"SO WHAT'S 'APPENING UP THERE?" asks Titch when Guja and I get out of the crawl space and meet up with him again underground. He's pacing back and forth like a bear in a zoo, occasionally thumping his meaty hands against the white tiles of the station walls. I figure he must be real tired of waiting in the subway.

"It's pretty nuts up in that bitch, I won't lie," I say. "Fortunately, that made it easy for us to get back. It's not like we're that much out of the ordinary because there is no ordinary."

The truth is, I don't know what to make of everything, except that things are looking pretty unpromising vis-à-vis world peace, if such a thing exists. We've tangled with Evan plenty, and he is my candidate for Person Least Likely to Be Responsible with a Nuclear Arsenal at His Command. So some Shit Definitely Has to Get Done. The question is, what shit exactly?

I have a sort of sinking feeling, like I'm in a scary new school or something. I realize how much I've been sustained by my friends, as if I only knew how to locate myself relative to other people—school, tribe, friendship, relationship. Now I'm on my own.

Well, that's not quite true. I have a killer giant and a lethal shrimp on my side. And, in a manner of speaking, I *am* still defined relative to another, which is to say, Chapel. I'm still in his gravitational pull.

Titch, however, seems a lot more positive than me.

"Right, then, Peter!" he says, clapping his massive hands together. I think he's trying to impress upon me a certain need for vigor. "Tell me what you know, and we'll see what we can do."

So we make our plan to defeat the Uptowners.

It's weird that everything seems to have conspired to make the Uptowners even *more* what they were. That is to say, these were the kids of the bankers, the lawyers, the hedge funders, the money people. The people everyone used to call the Masters of the Universe, way back in the day. They were raised to go to the best schools, get into the best colleges, get the best jobs at the best firms. They probably assumed they'd run things. And now it looks like they will.

But not if a black queen, a pint-size assassin, and the Cockney Mountain That Rides (the subway) have anything to do about it!

Fifteen minutes on, we're perched in the shadows near a line of chugging diesel generators. They're guarded by two Uptowners in camo, smoking up. Big cables run from the gennies along the ramp to the vaulted lower levels, where there's a chaos of junction boxes and extension cords and lamps that light the labyrinth. Kids are always stealing power without regard for the consequences to the rest of the grid, hence the technicians running to and fro trying to tweak the electrical flow.

I don't actually understand this stuff. Brainbox explained it to me when we escaped from here the first time, after the gladiatorial combat and the arms deal and cocktails at the Campbell Apartment. I miss those cocktails. I could have gotten used to the Bazaar, if it wasn't run by fascists.

I pat the sheet of paper in my pocket, where I wrote down Brainbox's final message. The launch codes. A farewell to the world, if one had the football and wanted to use it.

I walk over to the Uptowners. They eye me with suspicion and a soupçon of contempt, on account of I'm black and also because of their sophisticated gaydar, which is ever powerful in latent-homosexual private-school white boys.

"You boys know you shouldn't be smoking around these things," I say, walking past them and running my hand along the cowling of the foremost genny.

"Get your hands off that," says one.

"Diesel's not flammable, bitch," says the other.

"Oh, it's not *flammable*," I say, "but it is *combustible*. Which is almost the same thing. People think that diesel can't catch on fire. They're wrong." More science from poor Brainbox, to baffle these fools.

I'm doing a fairly good job of drawing attention my way, and I decide to amp it up a little by doing a spin and flourish, as if I were demo'ing the genny for a game show.

"What do you want, fag?" says the beefier of the two Uptowners.

I was almost feeling sorry for these chumps. So it's good that he said that because it makes it easier to live with what Guja does next. There's a tinny little hiss as his knife comes out of its scabbard, then a blur as he brings it down on the neck of the first guard. His head actually comes off, bounces on the shoulder of the other as he turns, which is worse for him, since he actually sees the blade as it sweeps through his neck in Guja's backhand cut. I half expect him to keep going and chop me apart, too—the look in his eyes is of some-body doing exactly what he always wanted to do—but instead, he whips the blade to the side, spattering a fine line of blood against the sandstone wall, which sucks it up like a wood stain.

"Jesus," I say. "Jesus, Mary, and Joseph."

"Very good, sir!" says Guja, and snaps to a sharp salute, his boots crashing together.

Titch emerges from hiding, hands out the goggles from his kit bag. They're the same kind we used long ago, back in the library. Hope it goes better this time.

"Right, then." Titch shuts down the first genny, and the lights start to go out. "Do the honors, Guja."

Guja goes down the rest of the line, and I can barely make out the figure of the Gurkha, bringing his blade down again and again, this time on the cables leading from the gennies, chopping off power for good. As they go offline, a localized quiet sets in.

I fire up the night-vision goggles, see Titch and Guja in their green irradiance as they do the same.

Shouts and cursing from below, down the length of the ramp. Some techs are already making their way to the first genny, flashlights in hand.

Guja strides down the corridor toward them, and I grab his arm. It's like a gnarled hardwood tree stump.

"They're just civilians, Guja," I say. "Get it? Just like you and me. Well. Just like me. Only the ones in camo are soldiers." I'm worried Guja is going to go buck-wild, take mad revenge for his homeboy he saw get shot.

"Them's the rules of engagement, Private," says Titch. "Let's not wear out our welcome, right?"

"I will be the best of guests, *sah*!" says Guja.

Titch and I slip past the techs, who are preoccupied with the generator anyway. It's pretty unlikely they'll be able to fix it, unless they have replacement cables, and Guja's role in the plan is to keep the lights out should that or anything else unforeseen happen. He'll monitor the lower-level floor and create enough havoc with the guards to take the heat off us, at least in theory.

In the ghost light of the goggles, the crowd at the lower level looks like the souls of the dead in Hades or something. Or that big poem where the Italian guy Dante goes through hell. Jefferson would know what I'm talking about. Which I guess makes me Virgil or whatever, and Titch is the guy who has to cross the river of hell in that Chris de Burgh song.

Flashlights are popping up here and there, but mostly it's people wandering around and bumping into each other. I slink between them, but Titch just barrels right through, knocking them on their butts.

We make our way through the lower level of the Bazaar to the far side, where two guards are waiting at the entrance to the Oyster Bar. Though the guards can't see better than anyone else, they're between us and the door, so we have to deal with them.

Behind us, we hear shouts and gunshots, which must mean that Guja is doing his thing. I say a little prayer for whoever is on the wrong end of that curved knife.

The guards start to drift toward the sound, which is bad news for them, since it gives Titch the chance to seize their heads, one face enveloped in each gigantic hand, lift them up, and slam them to the ground. He mashes them repeatedly into the tiles, and other than the cracking of their skulls, they don't make a sound.

We're through the doors and in the vaulted main chamber of the restaurant when we see the body hanging there. It's upside down, hanging from its ankles, a steady drip-drip from the top of its head. Titch gets hold of it and spins him round to face us. It's Wakefield.

Or it *was* Wakefield.

"Who's there?" someone hisses from the doorway to the bar-room nearby.

We turn, and Titch puts his finger to his lips. Then, with surprising agility, he slides over to the Uptowner making his way from the bar and brings his elbow down on the top of his head. The guy falls to the ground like the proverbial sack of potatoes. Actually, he seems to accordion downward rather than topple over. It's an uncanny, weirdly Slinky motion that reminds me of how the towers fell that day.

If Titch is sentimental about Wakefield, he definitely isn't letting it slow him down. He makes his way over to the glass porthole of the bar door and peeks through. Then he gestures to me to cover him. At least, I think that's what he does. He's using those cool hand gestures that people used to do in old movies about SEAL Team Six and whatnot. I figure it can mean only a few things, and the most likely is *Cover me.* So I raise my rifle and try to look like I know what I'm doing.

Titch abandons the quiet approach and slams through the door, his bulk taking it off the hinges.

There's only one person in the room, though. It's Chapel. He's tied to a chair, his hands behind his back. Next to him sits the football. Chapel is making silly trying-to-speak-through-a-gag noises, like he really wants to tell us something.

I rush over to him—and then stop.

Something's wrong.

He looks up at me and shakes his head, as far as the rope will allow him to. His mouth is stuffed with rags secured with twisted wire.

Titch leans over the football and picks it up.

He turns the briefcase upside down, and more rags fall out.

Something's *very* wrong.

I've fallen for the whole blinded-by-the-light thing before, a million years ago at the public library. So I rip off my goggles before they come on.

But Titch isn't so lucky. I can hear him grunt as the goggles overload and his eyeballs get clouded with information. He rips the goggles from his head and blinks as the Uptowner guards pop up from behind the bar and fire.

They've clearly been told to take out the biggest threat first. Titch staggers backward as the bullets pock his body. Then, as the Uptowners leap over the counter, he actually gets up and charges them, even though he's been hit maybe a dozen times. Titch seizes the first Uptowner to reach him and slams the guy against the bar, sending his gun flying. Someone swings a bat at him, but he catches it in his hands and yanks it away. But then he's stabbed from behind.

I shoot the kid who did it and try to run to Titch, but I'm tackled by a guard I hadn't seen come through the bar door. Another arrives and cracks me over the head with something unpleasantly hard.

As my head hits the ground, I see Titch among a crowd of Uptowners. They're bashing him with rifle butts and baseball bats, hacking at him with machetes. Like dogs around a bear, until finally he falls to his knees. Then they push him over and keep hitting him when he's on the ground, past the rattling of his breath, until he is quiet for good.

DONNA

WE'RE AROUND THE SIDE OF the front façade of the Museum of Natural History when the flare goes up, and Imani and half her team open fire on the front steps. The three guards at the entry are down in seconds. Half of Imani's Slayer Queens scramble across the street to flank the doorway, while the rest stay behind the park wall.

Bitchin'.

More guards issue from the front, beneath the weird-ass giant scorpion thing perched over the entryway. They fire back at the girls in the park, failing to see the girls to the side. More go down. The ones following them learn from their friends' mistake, duck back inside, and fire from the cover of the doorway.

Imani's team is doing its job, occupying the attention of the slavers. I have to admit I thought Imani, who seems kind of a bookish type, was going to leave the fighting to her all-female muscle, but she's leading the charge at the entrance, purple gun in one hand, loudspeaker gripped in the other.

She issues commands to the girls taking cover behind the parked cars across the street. The cars get riddled with little holes as someone in the recesses of the lobby opens up with a machine gun. Imani fetches a glitter-deco'ed hand grenade from her belt, pulls the pin with her teeth, and chucks it through the doorway. There's a blast, and smoke, and then Imani and her girls charge in.

That's our cue to sprint to the side door, about halfway down the block.

There's a chain and padlock threaded through the door handles, but Theo makes short work of it with a massive pair of bolt cutters. The chain pops and slithers to the ground.

The twins are in first, running ahead of us like it's a game. They won't even listen to Kath. Theo follows Kath, and then me, Jeff, and finally Rab, who does not look happy to be here. His pistol is clutched in his hands, his eyes darting around.

Me: "Watch it with that thing. I don't want any of us to get shot in the back."

He gives me a funny look, like I've caught him in something, then nods.

The lights are off in this part of the building, and Theo's headlight carves an angle into the blackness. The twins have climbed up the narrow stairs, and their voices bounce loudly back to us, giving us away to anybody who might be watching the entrance.

We discover them twisting and turning a big metal doorknob with no success.

"I got this," says Theo, and slaps the C-4 onto the doorframe, the clay-like block resting above the lock. Then he jabs an end of wire fuse into it and starts spooling it backward, making us turn and shuffle back the way we came. Down and around the corner of the stairs.

"Cover your ears," he says. "And scream when I tell you. Don't want the air pressure exploding your eyeballs or something."

This sounds bad, so we do as he says, and the boom of the explosive is preceded by a fearful caterwauling. Still, the abused air slaps down the stairwell and hits me like a full-body punch.

We get up from the ground, where we've been toppled onto each other, an awkward mingling of various love triangles that would take some working out if there weren't more important things to do.

We scamper as fast as we can in the darkness, along the cool marble corridor toward the Whale Room. Our footfalls echo in snaps and pings off unseen vaulting. Then, far ahead of us, a portico vomits light into the blackness.

There's a crowd of bearded slavers in the middle of the room, guns up, alerted by the attack on the front steps and our C-4 blast.

Behind them, girls are up at the windows of their enclosures, smacking their hands against the glass.

We back off, and I fire blind through the doorway, hoping I don't hit any of the display cases. We have to keep the slavers in the center of the room.

Perched at my shoulder, Jefferson slides a telescoping metal rod with a mirror on the end past the threshold of the portico. He's able to take a good look before a bullet smashes the mirror and sends the rod spinning along the floor, where it hits Rab, huddled against the wall with his hands over his ears.

It doesn't make me think less of him. If anything, seeing his usual above-it-allness brought low floods my heart with sympathy. No time for that.

Jefferson looks at the broken mirror.

Jefferson: "Bad luck for them."

He nods to Kath, who fires up the flare and tosses it into the room. It's NYPD traffic-division standard issue, glowing fuchsia, a nice touch.

That's the signal for the third team, up top.

Jefferson is muttering: *Namu amida butsu, namu amida butsu*, over and over again. His Buddhist stuff.

Then I hear a crack of distant thunder. A groan of metal, and a closer smashing, like a great wave crashing on a seawall. Dust sprays through the doorway.

Now's our chance. We rush in, guns raised, to see the famous blue whale, now fallen to the floor from where it hovered fifty feet above. A ninety-foot-long monster of fiberglass and polyurethane, it's smashed into two jagged pieces by the fall, like a great ship broken upon the rocks. Right on top of the slavers.

Some are still struggling to get out from under it, their legs shattered, screaming. Others are dead, impaled in bizarre poses by huge shards of fiberglass. Anyone left standing is covered in dust and particles, stunned and docile. They drop their guns to the floor, choke, raise their hands in surprise and submission.

A lot of the displays are broken, and girls burst from their pens, some of them seizing guns from the dead and wounded. I try to find Carolyn and the others, wandering through the clouds of dust.

Above, the Slayer Queens make their way to the upper balconies from the roof, which has been blown open by the explosive charge that brought down the whale.

In front of me, a familiar face. A rotund, pleasant-looking boy, his fake beard hanging from one ear, frozen in shock.

"Do you remember me?" I say to him. He looks like a statue, white with dust.

The boy says nothing at first, but then a look comes to his face. Recognition. And panic.

I put my gun to his chest and shoot him. He collapses to the floor.

I'm about to shoot another one of the slavers when Jefferson grabs me. We struggle, then fall to the ground. I look him in the eyes, and for a moment, I feel nothing but defiance, a challenge:

Tell me what I did was wrong. Then I burst into tears, and Jefferson holds me and hushes me like a child.

When I look up, I see Rab, standing near, a thin little dagger in his hand. He's looking at me—or is it Jefferson?

He's saying, "I can't. I can't."

I want to tell him it's okay—he can leave all the killing to us. That it's not a natural thing to do. That, anyway, these slavers are nothing to him. But the fact is, here, he'll have to get his mind around it. I hope that if it comes down to it, he'll do what he needs to do.

PETER

TITCH'S BLOOD HAS CONGEALED; his eyes have milked over. It's a mystery—the breath stops and then you're not you. I can't help but watch as he turns from a person to a thing, a body without a soul. Where's it gone? Maybe no place. That's what Brainbox said anyway.

Me, I was brought up differently: I believe that Titch is in the loving arms of Jesus. Of course, that image is just a metaphor, right? I mean, I can see him right here, so I don't imagine that there's also someplace where his real body is in the real hands of JC; that's just language messing things up, turning ideas into pictures. I can't help but look at Titch and shudder.

The other choice would be to look at Chapel, but I can't bring myself to do it. He's been making eyes at me for a while, like he could explain his betrayal away with sufficiently active eyebrows.

It's funny because at times I would have given anything to see him again. Now here we are, tied up in the center of the room, and I can't for the life of me think of anything to say. Maybe it's hate. Maybe it's love. Maybe it's the concussion.

"Peter." It's Chapel, who's finally managed to spit the rag out of his mouth.

I don't say anything.

"Peter. Look at me."

No dice. "You betrayed me. You betrayed all of us."

"You don't know the whole story."

Great. So next I'm supposed to say, *Then tell me the whole story*, all skeptical-sounding. But I don't feel like it. Even though I *want* to hear his voice.

"No more stories," I say. He knows what I mean. The story he had me believing in, where he loved me, and me and him were going to ride into the post-apocalyptic sunset.

But he starts telling his story anyway, and I don't have my hands free to block my ears, and it seems silly to drown him out by humming or whatever.

"Remember something," he says. "It wasn't me who screwed up Jefferson's Gathering."

"It was *your* Gathering. Your idea."

"No. I just knew what Jefferson wanted. That's all."

I can't disagree. It was Jefferson who always dreamed of Utopia. Like you could make lemonade out of apocalypse lemons, or a new society out of the secondhand pieces of what was left after What

Happened. So he went hook, line, and sinker for Chapel's suggestion of a Gathering of the Tribes.

"I was right about the Gathering," he says. "Look what's happened. What little social cohesion there was in this godforsaken place is going out the window."

"Don't pretend you care about that. All you care about is the nukes."

"They're the only way anybody here is going to live out the year. Trust me."

I look away from him, at the smashed mirror above the bar. Try to keep from crying. His body is warm against mine.

"That's funny," I say. "Trust you."

"Listen to me. This is all part of a plan. But if you don't help me get free, *everyone* is going to die. The Reconstruction is going to invade and liquidate the population."

"You're full of shit," I say. "Before, you said that they were going to leave us alone to die."

"Yes, *before*. Now they have a reason to come. Oh, they'll spare a few hundred, use them for medical stock. The rest of you they'll kill before you can do any more harm."

"What harm are we doing?" I say. I've had about enough of this bullshit from Chapel. Had about enough of the adults and what they want. Not for the first time, I wish we had never left Washington Square, hadn't gotten mixed up in this whole story.

I struggle against the bonds; the metal chairs creak but don't give.

"Do you know how the Reconstruction kept from getting infected, Peter?"

I don't. I figured they had a Cure, like us. But maybe that's not it.

"Quarantine..."

"No," says Chapel. "That was just a tiny part of it. Only for those who'd made it once everyone else had been taken care of."

I don't like the sound of "taken care of." It tends to mean the exact opposite.

"They shot them out of the sky, Peter. The airliners."

"How many?"

"*All of them.* Anything from the US. Then they blew up the ships—all the long-haul freighters. They missed things, here and there. There was an outbreak in Muscat, in Oman. A freighter had gotten through in error. Cases reported at local clinics."

His face twitches before he regathers his composure and tells me, "They nuked it, Peter. They cauterized it. Six hundred thousand people. A human firebreak."

I look at him. Try to find out if he's telling me the truth. Was this how he looked when he told me he loved me?

"I just want you to know the kind of people we're dealing with, so you'll understand what we've done."

God.

"What do you mean? What have you done? *What?*"

"We've had to even the playing field, Peter. If we didn't, they'd do the same here. Blow this city up, just to make sure that your Cure couldn't spread."

God.

"You're *insane*. Why wouldn't they want the Cure to *spread*?" He's said this kind of thing before, but I never bothered to question it because I was in love, which makes you stupid, I guess.

"Two reasons," says Chapel. "One, you're all incredible pains in the ass. Nobody wants to deal with a whole country full of teens. Two, you're all little breeding grounds for the virus."

"But the Cure—"

"It works for a while, Peter. But there's a phenomenon called antigenic shift."

I remember that phrase from the *Ronald Reagan*. Every time they took blood from us, they explained it was because of *antigenic shift*. But if you asked what *that* was, they said it was classified.

"Antigenic shift. When a virus mutates in the wild through genetic recombination. Usually, it's due to a leap from one species to another. But *this* one..." He means the Sickness. "We were able to tease a few new strains into existence. All it takes is a couple of people with the virus. If you've already had it and been cured, you're safe. If not, and you have last year's Cure, you're a sitting duck."

It takes me a while to figure this out. "You mean..."

"We needed to level the playing field, Peter."

I feel sick to my stomach.

"You didn't do it," I said.

"It wasn't just me doing it, Peter," he says. "Something like this takes a whole network of people. Hundreds. Thousands. And understand, these people are risking their lives."

"You infected the whole world." I can barely contain the idea.

"We did. Over a hundred agents, in over a hundred cities. By now, there's no way to quarantine it."

I can't breathe.

"It was the *only* way. The only way to save people. You understand? There are millions of kids left. Here, the rest of the country, all the way down south to Tierra del Fuego. The only way to save everyone is for everyone to be in the same boat."

"Everyone's infected…" I say to myself. I remember the chaos. The electricity going down. The food running out. Society rupturing.

"Nobody needs to die, Peter. The symptoms are only *starting* to show now. And they can develop cures for each of the strains. But to do that, they'll need your blood."

"*My* blood?"

"Who do you think we got it from? You and your friends. That'll be our export, Peter. The genetic information they need to make cures. In return, the rest of the world keeps us supplied, until we can set the country on its feet again. But none of this works unless we have the means to defend ourselves. That's why we need the football."

I understand. I'm not saying I agree. I'm saying I understand the idea. We have the Cure. We have the nukes. We need something to trade. And it's us. Part of us, anyway.

"Brainbox," I say. "You killed Brainbox."

"I *shot* Brainbox. I didn't mean to kill him. But he was trying to stop me from doing what I had to do, for the good of everyone else. I regret it. I wish that I had had time to explain. He wasn't well, Peter. He wasn't in his right mind. You know that yourself. And he had his hands on the nuclear codes and the football. I had to stop him."

I do remember how strange Brainbox was in the last days, how withdrawn and cold he had been since SeeThrough died. I wasn't there, to know if Chapel was telling the truth. But I do know that, with his last breaths, Brainbox didn't use the biscuit to hurt anyone. He used it to get help for his friends.

What can I do now, though? Now that I know. If the rest of the world is infected…If Evan still has the nukes…What can I do but help Chapel?

"Peter," he continues, "I'm sorry I couldn't tell you this before. I swore an oath. And nothing could make me break it, not even how I feel about you."

I push that thought from my mind. A last question occurs to me.

"Why?" I say. "Why do this for us?"

"Not just you," says Chapel. "All of us. Everybody who never had a chance. 'Your tired, your poor, your huddled masses yearning to breathe free, the wretched refuse of your teeming shore.' Do you know that poem? It was written by an American, Emma Lazarus. It's inscribed inside the Statue of Liberty. There are plenty of people who need land, and space, and resources, and they're willing to help a young country—a *literally* young country—get on its feet."

JEFFERSON

WHEN MY EARS CLEAR, I hear Imani, arrived from the front entrance, supervising her soldiers as they smash more of the diorama façades. Some of the captives need coaxing out, since all hope of rescue seemed to have evaporated before now, and it's hard for them to believe that we are not bringing some further torment to inflict on them. But here and there a familiar face, altered by time and hunger, appears, and we get our tribeswomen to reassure the others.

The girls we free from the ocean dioramas tell us there are more, many more, and we make our way through the vast building, making slow progress through the dark, doubling back again and again, interpreting the blueprint by flashlight and lighter.

The Hall of Mexico and Central America…the Hall of African Peoples…the Hall of Plains Indians. We work our way through all of them.

We come to a hall with two levels of dioramas and a herd of

taxidermied elephants in the middle, the bull's trunk extended in a silent call. The slavers make their last stand here, and the elephants are gradually pocked with new bullet holes (the original ones were, presumably, repaired).

From behind the dead wildlife, the surviving people emerge blinking, crying, tearless, voiceless, screaming. Finally, we have a parade of hundreds.

The Uptowners are next.

Carolyn, Donna, and I make a tally of our tribe members: Kristy, Shannon, Ayesha, Olivia, all three of our Ashleys. More and more. It starts to feel like a victory and not just a slaughter the farther we get away from the gruesome room with the blue whale spattered with blood.

"You took long enough," says Carolyn as she helps some girls out from where they were hiding behind a pair of black rhinos.

"I did," I admit. "I'm sorry."

"We thought you were dead when things broke up at the UN," she says. "Glad you're not."

"For now," I say. For all I know, we may be joining the black rhinos soon enough.

We've lost a single fighter, a tall girl named Lanita. She is laid in state on a wooden bench in the Hall of African Peoples, beneath a Zulu chief's cowhide shield, with a knobkerrie and assegai at her side. The freed girls pass by in a silent line, each touching her face in a grateful tribute before moving on.

In the very last room we search, we find some old friends. Tricia and Sophie, who we knew as Psychedelic Cowgirl and Morticia. At first, we miss them because, with their usual aplomb in matters of clothing, they have torn off the hides of the buffalo they were penned up with and turned them into warm ponchos.

"OMFG," says Cowgirl.

"WTAF," says Morticia.

"'Sup, Buffalo Girls," says Donna. "Won't you come out tonight?"

In the shadow of the herd of elephants, we try to decide what to do next.

Imani, flashing a rare smile, is all for keeping the momentum. "I say we roll on, take out the Uptowners. They're slippin' anyhow; that's what I hear."

"You won't get any argument from me," I say. "Let's hook up with our friends." I've been avoiding contact for now, not wanting to give Peter and the others away with a transmission at the wrong time.

"Only—I'm after something in particular."

Imani looks at me skeptically. "Go on."

I've been wondering what I would tell Imani, but the possibility of getting killed before it was even an issue had allowed me to punt the question downfield. Now I can either lie to her or give her information that could end up, if she plays her cards right, making her the most powerful person in the world.

There's the way Chapel played it. There's the way I played it before, when I knew the most important thing there was to know— I lied to Imani and everyone else.

So I decide to do the opposite.

"The Uptowners have a device," I say, "that controls the US nuclear arsenal."

Imani blinks.

"Okay," she says. "Explain."

So I do.

Or at least, I get partway in before Rab's walkie-talkie chirps.

"Come in," says Rab as we cluster around him.

Evan's voice comes over the line.

"To whom am I speaking?" The precision and formality of a true sadist.

"How did you get this?" says Rab. But I already know the answer. It's the channel we agreed on with Titch.

"I got it from your pet giant," says Evan. "Afraid he didn't survive the procedure."

Donna gasps and covers her mouth. She steps back, presumably to keep Evan from hearing her cry.

"Yeah, he took quite a while to finish off. Guy had a lot of guts. Anyhow. Let's talk."

"What about the others? Is Peter alive?"

"Is that the queer? Yeah, he's still kicking, for now. The other Brit is gone, though."

"I need proof that he's alive."

"Well, I would only give you proof if I wanted something from you. But I don't."

"You do," I say. "You do want something."

"What's that, Jeff?"

"You want to kill me." Donna looks at me like I'm crazy.

"All in good time," says Evan. "Remember, it's not really up to me. It's up to the guy in the sky."

Kath grabs the walkie from Rab.

"Evan?" she says.

"Oh, hi, Sis," says Evan.

"Evan, listen to me. If you let Peter go, I'll let you go."

"Let *me* go?"

"Yes. Instead of putting you down. Like I plan to."

"Words are air, Sis. Nice try, though. You've got balls. You should have been a dude. Well, gotta go. I'll be in touch."

EVAN

WELL, THAT WAS FUN. I wish I could be there and just watch them, just enjoy the utterly fucked expressions on their faces.

Me and the boys are moving out, heading along a damp, smelly maintenance corridor.

In a way, it's a shame I can't wait for them to arrive, which they will no doubt do, being the kind of friend-rescuing dickheads they are.

I wonder, for a second, if anybody would rescue *me*.

Maybe not.

Still, I'd trade any amount of palling around and shooting the shit for the feeling I have now, being on top of it all, kicking ass and taking names. Am I lonely? Sure. But we all are.

Gunfire from up top. That'll be the old folks, either the Russians or the Chinese, depending on who got here first. They've come for the football, of course. Oh, they'll probably wrap it up in some bullshit, like they're trying to prevent catastrophe, or save us from ourselves, or something, but when it comes down to it, they want the power and they don't want anybody else to have it.

My boys will slow them down, but there's only so much they can do. It was definitely time to abandon the old HQ. The Bazaar is done.

I don't care. The way I see it, this was just small potatoes, just a stepping-stone. All that matters is me and the nukes and the deal I'm going to cut with the Reconstruction people so that I don't make a deal with the Resistance or the Chinese or the Russians. Or maybe I *will* make a deal, if they have a better offer. *Somebody's* got to have something better than what that bitch Chapel wanted. I'm not going to hand over control to some Resistance so they can let a bunch of losers and mud people come in and ruin the country even worse than it's been ruined.

I kick open the door to the stairwell that leads up to the street level. And I ponder my next move.

What this place needs is a straight shooter like me in charge. And if people aren't smart enough to see that, I'll have to make it apparent myself.

See, yours truly is not as much of a dumbfuck as his teachers used to say. All those fuckers who said I wasn't meeting my potential? Turns out, I can do the reading when it's something I'm *interested* in. Like, for instance, the section of the football's documents headed *Strike Option Packages.*

It took me a little while to work out, but the tl;dr is this: You can't just launch a nuclear missile like it was a video game or something. There were some military guys who, like, simulated a whole bunch of scenarios and then programmed in shortcuts so that you could respond with a code, depending on what places you wanted to nuke. Those are the "packages" they're talking about. Like a meal combo at McDonald's.

Except, instead of ordering Double Quarter Pounder with Cheese Meal, you're ordering St. Petersburg and Vyborg, or Beijing and Tianjin, or whatever. All you have to do is know the activation code and have the biscuit to do it.

The door opens onto the street. I hear the rattle of gunfire from inside the terminal. Some kids are fleeing out the front doors. Good. More cover for us. I heft the black briefcase along.

The shit is kind of out of date, and the entry process is slow, which I guess they did so that fools couldn't launch a strike by accident like they were butt-dialing or whatever.

Anyhow, after a suitable period of study, I've decided to dial in a strike, just to show people that I mean business.

This probably sounds like I'm some kind of shitty James Bond villain—like, they were always threatening to nuke Paris *if* you didn't pay up or whatever. But what's different is (a) I'm cutting to the chase and actually blowing the place up and (b) I'm not stupid enough to blow up Paris or London or something. I mean, if you did that, they'd definitely have to take you out.

No, I'm going to blow up someplace so they know I'm serious about killing people, but someplace that the Reconstruction Committee clearly don't give that much of a shit about. So after much consideration, I have settled on Damascus and someplace called Homs. Nobody really cares about a bunch of Syrians, which is obvious enough from, like, world history. I mean, people might even *thank* me.

At the very least, they will know that I am not a guy to fuck around with.

Yes, I know that there are loads of, like, innocent people and women and children and whatever, but I've been getting along just fine without them, so I don't see why this should matter. And really, is it any different from how everybody else acts? I mean, if people cared more about the little kids and everything, at least more than all the other shit they care about, they would have done something about them already. Sure, when they die, they're all, like, boo-hoo. But up till then? Nothing.

I'm going to have to delay the launch, though, because I'm still waiting to hear back from the Reconstruction people. After I told them Chapel wasn't in charge anymore, they freaked out and said that they had to *form a response*, which I guess is their term for slow-playing and hoping that some of their commandos are still alive to try to kill me. I know they're going to reject my demand, which is to be acknowledged as the acting US head of state. Probably because of some bullshit like I don't command the allegiance of the populace or something. Which is true, except give me a second.

Uptown may be going through some hard times, but we're gonna stage a Bieber-level comeback. It's like when my man Adolf was back to the wall, hanging out in the bunker, and everybody was like, *The Führer has a secret weapon he's just waiting to use! It's gonna turn the whole war around!* Well, just imagine if he actually had nukes. Yeah. When people see that I brought the world powers to heel, you best bet they will kiss my ass.

Why else would that dude Kim Jong Whatever have made it as long as he did? He had a shitty haircut, he had zero charisma, but he had the nukes.

Now that I know I'm willing to kill, like, millions of people, it really puts everything else into perspective. I mean, what does it matter that I killed maybe twenty, thirty people personally, that my boys killed a lot more? It's refreshing to shake off any little vestiges of guilt that might have been floating around like toxins in my system. I mean, it's not like I ever *really* cared, but it's hard to shake the prejudices of your upbringing, right? Like the whole tiny-little-voice-that's-your-conscience bullshit. And maybe that's what growing up is: learning to be just who you are, not who other people want you to be.

Which is my way of saying that I don't feel bad about my plans to kill Chapel and the gay dude from the Square. Just satisfied that he came back for his little boyfriend. And I figure it's asking too much to bait the trap a second time, like expect to catch Jefferson the same way. So at this stage, the two 'mos are just an encumbrance.

But when I went back for them? They were gone. Bonds cut, no sign of them.

And I couldn't even take it out on the hides of the guys I left to guard them, because they're dead.

I'd like to do something about it, but it's not efficient at this stage to worry about how it all happened and how it's going to play out. I've got to keep my eyes on the prize. I can hear some kind of propaganda broadcast from inside the terminal, in English but with a telltale foreign accent.

"Put down your weapons. We mean you no harm. We have come to administer the Cure and restore order."

Yeah, right.

Me and my posse—my top twenty soldiers, who'll be, like, my Praetorian Guard in the New Order—cross Lexington, and over to the Chrysler Building.

It's all fortified and rigged up for power on the sixty-seventh floor. They called it the Cloud Club, and I figured the name was awesome, so I didn't call it anything new. When they built this building in the olden days, they made a special spot for the ballers and shot callers, because if you could build the tallest building in the world (at the time), you know you would put in a nice place to get your drink on with other rich white people.

The old place is pretty cherry, with cool murals of Pre-Sickness

New York seen from the air, marble columns, granite floors, and velvet chairs. A year ago, I had it stocked up with canned food and lots of booze so we can chill here for quite a while as the hoi polloi duke it out below. We even have an elevator powered by people, which is probably a major bummer if you have to spin the giant hamster wheel to get it up and down (not my problem).

After about half an hour in the damn elevator, we wedge open the doors to the club and breathe in the clean air, high, high above the burning and pillaging and rotting corpses. My chief mechanic, Tucker, sparks up the generator, and we set the champagne to chill in the fridges. I know people say you shouldn't celebrate in the fourth quarter, but they're all dead and I'm alive.

Chapel's phone thing beeps. I pick up.

"Yyyyello?" I say.

"Where is Chapel?" they say. It's the Reconstruction peeps.

"I told you, forget about Chapel. You're dealing with me."

"Is Chapel dead?"

"Honestly? No. At least not yet." No need to tell them much more than that.

There's a pause on the line. Then: "We will only negotiate with Chapel."

"So you're saying you reject my deal."

"We never considered any kind of deal with you. There is no negotiation."

I'm wondering why they put it this way, and I figure that they're keeping an eye on the PR side of the thing, like, *How will history look at it?* If it all goes to shit, they won't want to get caught having negotiated with a sociopath.

(Yours truly.)

But so what? Like empathy is such a good thing? I read this book once (okay, I skimmed it) that said that lots of CEOs and stuff were sociopaths. But the author acted like that was a *problem*. The fact is that to get things done in life, you need to keep from having your viewpoint contaminated by other people's feelings. Would America have started if, like, George Washington was worried about how the British felt? No way. So I don't *feel* what other people are feeling. So I have to guess based on other factors. So I don't find emotions contagious. Does that make me a *thing*, the way Mom said it that last time? Fuck that noise.

However, the Reconstruction dudes clearly have no plans to deal with me. So as I expected, I'll have to convince them of my bona fides.

"Guys, I'm sorry to hear that. Looks like I'll have to demonstrate my goodwill or whatever. I'd check the news feed in about an hour or so if I were you."

They think they have room to maneuver. But their soldiers are dead. And nobody else can get to me up here.

So I hang up. And I fetch out the football. And my magic satphone. And I get to raining death.

KATH

THERE ARE PEOPLE RUNNING FROM THE Bazaar, and people running toward the Bazaar, and the *snap-crackle-pop* of gunfire tells me that the running-awayers are afraid of dying and the running-towarders are afraid of missing out on free shit they can loot.

I hope that Evan is okay.

If he's dead, I won't get to kill him myself.

When we enter from Vanderbilt Avenue, the first thing that hits us is the smell of gunshots. I look down onto the Grand Concourse from the balustrade. There's a battle going on between two squads of oldies—I think they're the Chinese and the Russians—and people are ducking and crabbing in the detritus. Bodies are scattered everywhere among the abandoned stalls like Death is scattering seeds. Around the edges, randoms and scavengers are scampering.

We watch as the two squads destroy each other. Finally, they drag their wounded off, down the ramps to the lower levels.

"Well," I say, "it's over."

"How do you figure that?" says the black girl. Oh, okay, *Imani*.

"Uptown's gone."

"That's not 'over' in my book. That's just a start."

Then out of the shadows below, a crew of weirdos in long robes filters in.

They walk up the stairs toward us, as Imani's girls level about a hundred rifles at them. The leader reaches up to his hood for some kind of video-game-trailer-type reveal.

Imani orders the guns down when she sees that it's Peter.

"Relax, y'all," he says. "It's just me."

Donna puts her gun down and goes over to hug him.

Peter laughs and says, "Check it out, I'm a prophet! The Ghosts saved me! And they gave me this cool robe."

Donna says, "You're famous, Peter. Congratulations."

I raise my hand. "Um, 'scuse me, but are these people who I think they are? Don't they, like, *eat* people?"

As I'm saying this, all the "Ghosts" seem to peep Jefferson for the first time because they go down on their knees and bow.

Dude. What the Actual.

"Lord..." One of the Ghost guys—their leader, I guess—dares to look up at Jefferson. "Lord, forgive us. We were mired in evil. We lost the true path... We were deceived by the enemy. We—"

"Get up," says Jefferson sharply. He doesn't seem that thrown by the way they're talking to him. Maybe it's because of how he got treated at the Gathering. Peter told me everybody was totally kissing his ass.

They get to their feet.

"Look," says Jefferson. "There's nothing special about me. I don't know much more than anybody else."

The Ghosts look confused. They were expecting more of a religious experience or something.

"Listen to me," he says. "You did wrong. We all did wrong, more or less. But you have a chance to do right now. We need your help. Then maybe you can get started on a better life. Understand?"

They stand there and sort of let that sink in. Then the leader nods, which I guess goes for all of them.

Meanwhile, one of the robed dudes has been standing the whole time.

"Good speech," he says. "My thoughts exactly."

That's when Chapel reveals himself, and up go the guns again.

He and Peter spend a long time explaining some mumbo jumbo about how Chapel might be a devious sack of shit, but he has the best interests of humanity in mind or something. Which is not 100 percent convincing, if you ask me, but it appears that there's not much time to make fine moral distinctions.

To cut to the chase, it turns out that Evan is alive and kicking, holed up someplace called the Cloud Club and up to his usual mischief. I mean, I guess it's more than his usual mischief—more like thermonuclear war.

The Ghosts mostly keep to themselves, conferring in hushed voices. Occasionally, one of them will do this weird thing where they run up to me, turn their back, and make this sort of squeezing motion with their fingers. After a while, I realize it's what we used to call taking a selfie, except with no camera phone. Like it's become this weird little series of ritual motions that don't end up in an actual photo because it doesn't need to.

Meanwhile, Imani announces that she's done her piece now that the Bazaar is liberated and the power of the Uptowners broken.

"The slavers and Uptowners beaten in a day," she says. "I think I'll win the next election."

Donna says, "We can't ask you to go any further..."

Imani says, "Then don't." But she smiles.

Jefferson puts his hand out to shake. "Thank you," he says.

"Not good enough," Imani says. "This is how you can thank me. This thing rolls your way, me and mine need a seat at the table. Understand? If not, we'll be coming for you."

"I understand," says Jefferson. And Imani shakes his hand.

So it looks like we've lost most of our muscle. Imani and her girls set to clearing out the Grand Concourse, securing the building, and sending messengers up to Harlem to spread the news.

I get a funny feeling in my chest, like the feeling when you want something really bad? But know you won't get it. Missing somebody.

Which is weird, because it's not like me and the Harlemites have ever been on the best terms. It's probably because, without the girl soldiers on our side, we don't have a fighting chance against the rest of my brother's posse. All we have are some half-starved slave girls and ex-cannibal freaks.

The rest of us set out for the Chrysler Building, spiky top glittering in the winter sunlight.

I feel a familiar presence at my side, and I turn and see Theo walking along, his eyes on the ground. He's left Imani and the Harlemites to lock down the Bazaar.

My face flushes, which is weird.

"You didn't say good-bye," he says.

"Looks like I didn't have to," I say.

Behind me, I hear giggling. It's the twins, who seem to be enjoying some kind of private joke. They keep looking at me and Theo and whispering.

We walk along some more, rounding the sandstone corner of the building, and it's really annoying because something is going on health-wise, too. My heart is like DunDUNdunDUNdunDUNDUN. Like I need a heart murmur on top of all this crap.

I turn to Theo and say, "Why did you come?"

He laughs. But then he looks back down at the ground, kind of angry.

"You know the answer," he says. And he looks back at me.

I remember the first time I met him. We were walking through Harlem, hoping to make our way to the East River Drive without getting shot. A full-on police car pulled up, sirens blazing, and we had to Assume the Position. In the patrol car on the way to head-quarters, hands cuffed, I looked at the back of Theo's head, a long horizontal scar across his bunched neck. And I told him to just go ahead and do what he was going to do.

But it wasn't like that.

Theo wasn't like that.

He was quiet and fierce and almost shy, his voice so low you had to strain to hear it.

Then later the twins and I found him tied up in a hangar on Long Island, and we got him free, and we boosted cars and road-tripped back to the city. He saved my life right back, in a pharmacy some-place on the Montauk Highway.

I figured I'd never see him again after we arrived at the UN. I was off to find Jefferson, and Theo was spreading the word that there was a whole other world, with electricity and food and run-ning water.

And he was back to Harlem, and I was back to whatever it is that I think I'm doing.

But why is my heart doing that?

Mom and Dad would not approve.

Mom and Dad are dead.

What if everything—the running and killing and starving and surviving the Sickness, even falling for Jefferson—what if it was to get me *here*? And now. With Theo.

My heart is still going DunDUNdunDUNDUNDUN.

This could be a bad idea. He could change his mind. He could walk away. He could get killed. He could get me killed. This could be a bad idea.

"I'm glad you came," I say, and I reach out and put my hand in his.

DONNA

I'M LOOKING UP at the shining eagles and giant winged hood ornaments studded around the top stories of the Chrysler Building, light winking down from the off-white sky.

Getting a real deathy vibe here.

I mean, there's *always* a chance you're gonna get your ass killed in this place; but it feels like things are particularly coming to a head at this particular moment. I wish we could just call it a day and head back to the Square to lick our wounds.

But Chapel says that if we don't get control of the situation fast, there'll only be more soldiers on their way, and the next time it'll be a full-on invasion.

The gist of it seems to be that Chapel and his Resistance buddies have infected the rest of the world with new strains of the virus they got out of us, me and my peeps, on the *Ronald Reagan*. Strains that they can't cure without access to our blood to make serum. The Resistance's idea is to keep curing and infecting the world in perpetuity, with new sources of virus from the citizens of Newest York and the rest of the United States of Post-Apocalyptic America. Or at least, they'll keep doing it until some kind of treaty can be signed. Keep them on a biological leash. We're gonna make this a new country of refugees and castoffs and escaped debtors and plague kids.

Our chief export? Our bodily fluids, to make serum, to keep the rest of the world healthy. Gross.

But the only thing that's going to keep the Reconstruction from tracking us down, imprisoning us, and hooking us up to pumps like dairy cows is the threat of the football. Which Evan is holding hostage in some cloud chamber up on the billionth floor.

So up the Chrysler Building it is.

We head down Forty-Second from Grand Central, under the green street overpass, trailing a herd of freed slaves. Some come from the Square but many from all over, and most of them will be absolutely zero use to us in a fight. Tired, traumatized, and hungry, they're following us for no other reason than that they don't know what else to do. In terms of able bodies, we've got me, Peter, Chapel, Jeff, Kath, the twins, Theo, and Rab. Carolyn and the Three Ashleys from our tribe have picked up guns from the dead commandos. That's about a dozen guns against however many Evan has left up there.

Can't wait them out, though. Kath says they have enough

food to last for months. Besides, Evan can get into some major, world-changing shit in a heck of a lot less time than that.

We leave the freed girls outside, under the command of Carolyn and the Ashleys. If any rescue party comes for Evan, they'll try to fend them off. And we go in through the formerly shining doors, now blotchily oxidized.

Rab comes up to me in the art deco hallway of the lobby, which is wall-to-wall marble, with slashes of bronze and burly murals.

Rab: "This elevator idea is insane."

Me: "Have you got a better idea?"

Rab: "Yes. Going home. Letting the big boys handle this. It'll be a complete massacre if we go up there. They're going to see us coming. They have half an hour to point their machine guns just the right way."

Me: "So you just want the Reconstruction to come in and sort things out, is that right?"

Rab: "That's absolutely right."

Me: "And what happens to us?"

Rab: "We'll be all right. We'll talk our way out of it. You can't think *that* lunatic"—he means Chapel—"and his bunch of anarchists are going to make anything better!"

Me: "You want me to trust the government."

Rab is desperate, pleading. His big gray-green eyes well with tears.

Rab: "Trust me. Trust *me*, Donna. I have seen all sides of this thing. And all I want is for you and me to be together. Your friends can come, too. I can arrange it. I know I can."

Me: "My friends? Even Jefferson?"

Rab pauses. Nods, as if he's debating with himself and has just come to an agreement.

Rab: "If I had wanted Jefferson to die, all I would have had to do is follow orders."

I realize he's telling the truth. He tries to take my hand. I pull it away.

Rab: "I did it for you. Or rather, I didn't do it. For you. For you to be able to *choose* who you want to be with. Choose me. Please. And we all live. We can go someplace safe and decent and peaceful. Come back with me."

I look at his beautiful face; I dream back to the time in Cambridge, quiet afternoons on the river, lazy mornings in Nevile's Court, the sun streaming in through the basement window. Some part of me plays a little movie of Rab and me, home again, safe and sound and happy.

Me: "That's just it. Rab, I'm not safe and I'm not decent and I'm not peaceful. This is me. This is my city. Our city. And nobody is going to take it from us. You can't understand that because you don't belong to anybody but yourself. You're not part of anything. That's why I can't love you." I watch the impact on his face.

It knocks the tears loose. "I'm sorry. I thought for a while I did. And I'm grateful for the time we had. It helped me then. But if you can't help all of us now, you had better go."

So he does. He nods and makes his way sadly out of the building.

JEFFERSON

THERE'S A SORT OF giant metal Ferris wheel that looks like it runs one of the elevators. It's big enough for three people to walk upward in an endless curved staircase, and others to help turn it using handholds on the rim of the big circle. The revolutions turn a gear that transmits friction to the elevator cables. It's not exactly efficient, but that's not a concern when you have slave labor, which the Uptowners did. Now it's abandoned, and the Uptowners made the mistake of leaving it intact.

I turn to Gamma, the lead survivor of the Ghosts.

"We're going to need you to power this."

"Your wish is my command, Lord. You go up to battle demons in the clouds. It is fitting."

"Look," I say. "You're not a genie, and I'm not the Second Coming. If we lose up there…" I gesture vaguely toward the ceiling.

"They're going to be after you. Understand? So you can't do this because I *said* so. You have to do this of your own free will."

He looks at me, uncertain. Then, "Okay."

"What's your name?" I say. "Your *real* name."

Again a pause. "Edward."

"Okay, Edward. Take it from me. Nobody and nothing else is the final authority except you. People are just people. We're all we've got to go on. Okay?"

"Okay."

I don't know that the Ghosts will have enough energy to actually get the elevator up there. But then the girls we freed start grabbing ahold of the wheel, handhold or no.

"We'll get it done," says Cowgirl. "Many hands, light work, that sort of shit. NP."

I notice a vacuum of silence nearby and see Rab walking off.

Things are looking up.

As we finish gearing up, I go over to Donna.

"You okay?"

Of course I don't really mean that. I mean, *What just happened?*

She just looks up and kisses me. "I love you," she says.

"I love you." Natural as breathing.

"Good," she says. "Now let's go save the world again."

EVAN

IT'S HARD TO BELIEVE THEY'RE SO STUPID.

About half an hour ago, my bro Monster says he's watching the needle on the elevator dial and it's moving up. Really slowly, of course, because the damn elevator is heavy and there's only so much the hamster wheel can do to lift it. That means that there's plenty of time to prepare for them.

It's definitely not my dudes in the elevator—they would know better and signal ahead of time. It's got to be Jefferson and his assorted half-breeds, sexual deviants, and losers.

How do I know? It just makes sense. Because I realize now that not only am I God's favorite show, I am his favorite *person*. And he is shaping my triumph. Now is the part where I beat back the mutated hordes and put the crown on my own head.

It's all working out! The champagne is chilling, the nukes are warming up, and my enemies are literally delivering themselves to me in a box.

The only disappointment is that last part. It's a tiny bit of a bummer that it's going to be so easy to kill Jefferson, after all this time. I briefly toy with the idea of engineering some kind of final showdown, like we take them captive and walk them off the silver eagles one by one so I can watch them fall all the way to the ground and hear the screams. We could even record it to play back whenever we want later. Put it up on YouTube once we get Wi-Fi back.

But I decide to be reasonable. So we just set up the flamethrower in front of the elevator, ready to incinerate them the moment the doors open. It's straightforward, a little blunt, maybe, but it's got a certain style. Maybe we can put them out before they're totally gone. That could be fun. I tell my boys to get the fire extinguishers.

I have the flamethrower in my hands, a little tongue of fire licking upward from the spout, when I hear the *DING!* of the elevator finally arriving. I have to shush the bros, who have all gathered around to see what it'll be like. Monster and the boys have their guns ready in case Jefferson and the others escape the elevator while they're on fire, and try to hug us to death or something.

As soon as the doors are half open, I give it the juice, and a chameleon-tongue of flame leaps out and into the elevator. By the time the doors are totally open, the elevator is engulfed, an aquarium of fire.

But I don't hear any screams, which is a letdown.

Then, as the flames die down, leaving only a few scraps licking at the corners, I realize that there's nobody inside.

That's when the grenade skitters into the landing and bounces off the back wall. I jettison the flamethrower and hit the ground just as it explodes, splashing me with what's left of Monster.

Looking up, I see that about half my guys are down, dead or writhing, but the others are firing back toward the Downtowners, who tricked us, I realize, into paying attention to the elevator while they legged it up sixty-seven flights. We might have had somebody guarding the stairway, but everyone wanted to watch our enemies get set on fire. I guess that's the downside to enabling a culture of sadism. People lose focus.

Time for a quick assessment of the position. About half my men are down, but the rest, perhaps aware of the fact that they'll be fighting for their lives, are up and gunning. An unknown number of enemies, but they've just hiked sixty-seven floors, so they have to be pretty tired.

Somewhere out there, Jefferson.

The flamethrower is out of commission, the tank punctured by shrapnel. The football, however, seems to have made it through. I grab hold of the leather handle of the briefcase and crawl to a side door to the club kitchen, avoiding the trouble.

They've shut off the generator, so the kitchen is dark and the fridge is silent. Before anything else, I open the fridge and take out a bottle of Cristal. Smash it open on the counter edge. I realize that I've made a mistake. God just gave me the thumbs-down on the latest plot twist, like how could I just flambé my archenemy?

So while the sounds of battle ring and pound from outside, I raise the bottle and chug. It's still cold, and as the champagne slides down my throat, I think to myself—it's a moment of weakness, I admit—of how cool everything could have been, how awesome if only Jefferson and the rest of those losers hadn't gotten mixed up in my story.

What if it's actually Jefferson? What if it's his story? That would be so lame.

Then, as the buzz of the champagne sets in, I remember the crushed Adderall I still have in my back pocket. I hold the baggie right to my nose—no time to be delicate—and huff it all in one breath like a sob.

Then the Adderall hits and I get a surge of energy, triumphant and creative, and I feel much better.

The big guy still loves me. That's why I'm still alive.

Of course it's me. Of course.

Now I know what I have to do.

PETER

I AM NOT EXACTLY *INTO* FIGHTING, but the fact that I am gay does not prevent me from kicking ass. As a matter of fact, I probably had to fight more than most kids. So when I see Chapel go down, my first instinct is not to run to him or to run away but to kill the guy who shot him. Which, you know, I do.

The rooms of this crazy old nightclub or whatever are filling up with smoke. I duck round a corner and fire into a mural wall, behind which I figure he's hiding. A moment later, I hear a groan, which is good enough for me. I lean over Chapel.

"Leg," he says. I drag him to some cover. I undo the straps from my pack and make a tourniquet, cinch it tight.

"I'm fine. Go help the others."

"Nope," I say. "Not leaving you alone. Last time I did that, you disappeared on me."

"I'm here to stay."

I hold his hand to my cheek, then return to the fray.

DONNA

FIRE AND MOVE. WE CRAB-WALK through acrid smoke, the painted clouds all around us. I get the drop on an Uptowner, coughing as he pops in a magazine, and fire a burst with my own gun. He disappears into the haze.

Then, before I can react, another comes screaming out of that same smoke, baseball bat raised. But as the kid swings, the bat meets Jefferson's sword and splits in two. The nub of the bat clatters musically across the floor, and the Uptowner turns and runs.

Finally, it's only us. Me, Jeff, Kath, Theo, and the twins peer through the smoke; Peter is over by a prone Chapel. I notice a channel of clear, cold air through the smoke, a draught from a pair of tall paneled French windows open to a wide terrace.

We walk through the threshold, and beyond the terrace, I can see the silvery nape of a giant eagle gargoyle jutting out from the corner of the building. And poised on the head of the eagle, against the city far below, is Evan.

He's holding the football to his chest like a baby. He looks deranged, his eyes wide.

Evan: "This is good. This is a good twist."

We walk out onto the terrace, rifles up, a half-dozen barrels pointed at him.

Evan: "You should know that if I go, the world goes with me."

Jefferson puts down his gun and his sword, steps forward.

Jefferson: "What do you mean, Evan?"

Evan: "I mean, *Jefferson*—nice to see you, by the way—that I've entered the launch codes for an attack on China and Russia. The nukes are warming up now. Fifteen minutes and they launch. You kill me, and the football falls sixty-seven floors. No chance of turning off those silos. Bye-bye, everything."

I get a flash of the puppets and their shadows on the screen. And I realize, to Evan, we're *all* just shadows.

I figure if there is anyone who could do what he's threatening, it's him.

Up high like this, it feels like the cold wind wants to tear the flesh off your bones. I see the clusters of building tops all around, birds wheeling in the distance.

Me: "What do you want?"

Evan: "What do I want? I want a lot of things. Mostly right now

I want to keep living. But in terms of what I think you can give me...I want *him*."

He points at Jefferson.

Evan: "You and me, Jefferson. You try to take the football. I try to throw you to your death. Just you and me, no weapons. Seem fair?"

Jefferson: "What if you win?"

I jerk my head toward him. I can't believe he's considering it.

Evan: "If I win? I don't know. Then I figure out what I want next. I don't think you're in much of a position to bargain, though."

Me: "Don't—"

But he steps forward, up and onto the silver neck of the eagle.

EVAN

HE GOES FOR IT, LIKE I FIGURED he would, and steps up onto the gargoyle. Time for the big showdown.

Except not. I get the club out from the waistband at the small of my back and bring it down nicely across his temple, and he crumples on the metal neck of the gargoyle, barely holding on. I shrug off the football to let it sit behind me and slip out the boot knife. I hold the point to his neck.

Now what? Well, I've marginally improved my bargaining position, and I'm definitely enjoying the prospect of beheading Jefferson.

Sure, I've sacrificed a lot of credibility. But I wasn't lying about the football. The nukes are all revved up! Billions of people don't know that they're toast. And nobody can stop it without the codes.

The roundness of it! The closure. I remember the moment we met, a bulletproof Plexiglas bus window between us, me with a pig on a leash, him speaking for his tribe in place of his older and smarter brother.

Now here he is, held in my arms, just where I wanted him all this time, with my knife at his throat.

I look down to figure out how best to start cutting—by the jaw-line? across the Adam's apple?—when some other guy hits me.

Head buzzing, I register somebody I haven't seen before, another one of Jefferson's brown people, almost as good-looking as me. He knocks me back again and away from Jefferson before I have time to react.

I hear someone scream, "Rob!" or something.

The guy has both hands on my wrist, trying to keep me from using my knife, which frees me to bash him in the face with the other hand. Meanwhile, he's shouting to Jefferson to get the foot-ball. Funny accent.

We start rolling off the edge of the gargoyle, and he has to let go of my arm so that he can stop himself. So I stab him in the chest and use his body to push myself up, which drives the blade deeper into him.

He's not dead, though, and it looks like he has a knife of his own—a little letter-opener-looking thing. He jabs me in the leg, and I fall to one knee. He kicks me in the stomach, and I feel myself lose purchase. I realize with a sick feeling that I'm about to go over the edge.

It can't be. It can't be. This is my story.

I can't die. God! I can't get canceled!

I'm slipping farther. I grab at the bronze of the gargoyle, but my hand is slick with blood, and then I'm falling…

But there's some consolation. I grab ahold of my attacker's leg as gravity sucks at me.

He falls down with a bump on the metal plating of the eagle and then, finally, painfully, we go over.

We are both flying now, floating down toward the city. For an insane moment, he looks me in the eye and we see each other, two souls in free fall, and I almost feel, although we've never met except to kill each other, as though we might be friends, in another life, if I were a different person.

And I think maybe it could have all been different, but of course it's too late.

DONNA

THERE ISN'T MUCH TIME TO MOURN. I look over the side, and thank God, I can't see the sidewalk below. I know Rab is dead. I will cry later.

I get the football by its handle, pull it to safety. Chapel has dragged himself over the threshold from inside and is shouting, "We need the access codes!"

I look over Peter's shoulder as he tears open the worn black briefcase. Inside is a satellite phone . . .

And an empty binder.

The launch codes are gone.

I fall to my knees. Now it's time to cry.

PETER

DAMNED IF I'M NOT GOING TO be famous after all. I don't mean, like, as "Saint Peter." That's just fame by association. That's just famous for being famous.

I run to where Donna's got the football. She's crying about the missing launch codes. Apparently once Evan realized we'd win, he wasn't going to let the world live past him.

Now my big fear is that if the biscuit—the little satphone thing with the link to the arsenal—is gone, there's nothing we can do.

I find it intact, tucked into a pocket in the briefcase. Win!

I let them all wallow in despair for just the tiniest moment, I admit. Check out the lost and forlorn looks on their faces as they ponder the end of everything. So I can make my entrance.

Then I pull the paper from my pocket. The codes Brainbox dictated to me, out of his supernatural memory.

His last message to the world.

I hand them to Chapel, who seems to know exactly what they are. He parses through the list, looking for a particular sequence.

He takes the biscuit from my hand and starts punching in numbers with great care.

I realize that if I didn't manage to write down the codes correctly, this isn't going to work.

Same if Brainbox got it wrong. Or if he told me the wrong codes on purpose. Why would he do that? Maybe for a moment like this, to show his contempt and disillusionment.

Maybe his last message is a big raised middle finger. Maybe he was trolling all of us.

At last, with a surprisingly everyday sound, like a laundry machine announcing its cycle is done, the biscuit signals that the launch has been aborted.

Chapel closes the leather flap on the biscuit and sinks back down to the ground, his energy seemingly spent. And Donna and I get to work on his leg.

I'm gonna be famous for saving the world.

"Good work," I say to Chapel.

He smiles.

"Now put your hands behind your back," I say. "You're under arrest."

JEFFERSON

WE PUT OUT THE FIRES on the sixty-seventh floor. It seems like a good way to begin things.

Then we make our way back down to the world again, with Old Man Chapel as prisoner. The young world isn't going to start with Brainbox's murderer free. If Chapel can prove his good intentions, we'll let him go.

The Ghosts and the freed girls are waiting at the bottom of the stairwell, even though I told them they should go once they'd finished sending us up. I ask them all their names—their *real* names.

Imani's Slayer Queens have secured the Bazaar. She seems a little surprised to see us, but I think she's pleased. I ask her if she'll help figure out how we're going to run things from now on. There's an awful lot to organize. Negotiations with the Reconstruction Committee. Distribution of the Cure. Policing. Civil services. Food supplies. Contact with other survivors in distant cities.

Meanwhile, we look for someplace to rest. Me and Donna.

DONNA

RAB'S SEND-OFF IS A VIKING funeral in Central Park, his body laid on top of branches in a rowboat floating in the Harlem Meer.

Chapel is already in negotiation with the Reconstruction, with Imani at his side, holding the satphone to his head. She's smiling. It's a nice smile.

Soon, technicians, builders, doctors, academics, workers from Syria and Iraq and West Africa will begin arriving, coming to help us rebuild.

I look around at the mourners. Kath and Theo are cute as heck. Maybe they'll even straighten out their two little psycho kids.

And Peter. I remember when I asked him to come along on a little recce up to the public library. And he said he was down for it 'cause he needed to meet new people. Well, he did. He's even got his own entourage. After all, he's a celebrity now.

The smoke from Rab's pyre joins the sky, where all the other fires expend themselves. Falcons wheel; dragonflies skim the surface of the water.

Myself, I wonder if Jeff and I can rebuild what we had. Can we go back to the moment on the boat, long ago, when we told each other how we felt? Or a morning in Washington Square, when we were just your average carefree post-apocalyptic teens? Or go even further back, to some point before the Sickness, before we lost so many people, and life held out a different promise?

No. But we can go ahead.

Night is coming. But then morning comes.

ACKNOWLEDGMENTS

Many thanks to Alvina Ling, Jill Yeomans, Nikki Garcia, Farrin Jacobs, Bethany Strout, Kristina Aven, Nellie Kurtzman, Andrew Smith, Jennifer Corcoran, Victoria Stapleton, Melanie Chang, and everyone at LBYR who have made this such a happy experience for me. Also to Suzanne Gluck, David Lubliner, and David Wirtschafter of WME, as well as my redoubtable cousin and lawyer, Alex Kohner.